Estranged from her parents, fifteen-year-old Gina Laramee longs to understand her family roots and to have a normal, loving relationship with her mentally unstable Aunt Elaine, since Elaine is the closest thing to a mother Gina has—and is in fact closer than Gina realizes.

Fed up with Elaine's drinking and verbal abuse, Gina flees to New York City's (1980s) Lower East Side in a half-hearted search for her mother, Ellen, who, according to Elaine, vanished into its underbelly after Gina was born. Instead of finding Ellen, Gina meets a group of artists. When they share their food, drugs and squat with her, she believes she's found her family at last—even when they pressure her for sex.

When Gina phones Elaine to say she isn't coming home, Elaine realizes she must atone for her mistakes. But before she can do this, she must confess the terrible secret she's kept from Gina.

At Elaine's tearful insistence, Gina agrees to meet, possibly for the last time, at a Times Square diner, where Elaine divulges the secret that changes everything Gina thought she knew about herself, Elaine and life.

So Nice to Finally Meet You...

by

Amy Laprade

Acknowledgements:

I want to thank the following folks who've contributed to this project:

Paul Richmond, Kathy Dunn, Don Fisher, Dorothy Goldstone, Alice Thomas, Eve Brown-Waite, Hazel Dawkins, Geoff Blüh, Dawn Spaulding, Janis Greve, Drew Hutchinson, Maria Louisa Arroyo. Kiana Davenport, Hye Young Chyun, Cheri Knight, Scott Borofsky, Sean Stedman, Matt Stedman, Jamie Finlay, Michael Free, Boo Pearson, Philippe Guy Simon, Don McAulay, Junko Suzuki Parsons, Cyclub band, the Flywheel Arts Collective, Christian Messman, Jay and Teresa (longtime residents of New York City's Lower East Side), David Ryan, Stephen O'Connor, Stephen O'Connor's Fact and Research in Fiction, Nonfiction and Poetry workshop, Olivia Warden, Matt De La Peña, Gotham Writer's Advanced Fiction workshop, Justin Taylor's fiction workshop, Bob Kanen, Dave Hunter, Judith O'Kulsky, Kevin O'Connell, David Detmold, Local Bias, KQED San Francisco Television Network, Edinburg Castle Pub, Bing Arts Center, Springfield Public Library, Art Space, Black Sheep Cafe.

Portrait by Geoff Blüh, hair by Cathy Flood, makeup by Hannah Tsutsumi.

This book is dedicated to Helen O'Kulsky Reed, Anne McGrath, Wilfred and Evelyn Laprade, Clifford Grover and to Isabelle Grover who continues to be a loving force in my life.

Published by Human Error Publishing
www.humanerrorpublishing.com
paul@humanerrorpublishing.com

ISBN: 978-0-9833344-5-3

Cover Photography by Dawn Spaulding

Cover Design
by
Amy Laprade and Paul Richmond

Table of Contents

"Duh...I'm Gina Laramee!" Chad, the scrawny kid who always sits at the back of the bus and has eyes like poached eggs, moans in a Neanderthal voice as he pelts me in the head with something small but hard.

Telling them off'll only make it worse, I remind myself while holding my gaze on the trees that zip past. They've turned this crazy, hunter's vest-orange overnight. It's like Mother Nature got bored or something, and decided to dot the hills with her paintbrush.

"Dude, she like, must be totally fucking retarded," clucks Barb, "An inbred. Look at her rotten teeth."

My cheeks burn like the leaves on the trees and I chew my bottom lip as their laughter fills every space of the big but claustrophobic bus before slapping itself down on the empty space next to me—on the green, vinyl bench seat, where there'd be plenty of room for another person to sit, yet no one in their right mind would ever sit next to Gina Laramee. With my tongue, I trace the tooth that'd turned gray from the time I flipped over the handlebars on my bike. I was ten, and my aunt and me were living with her boyfriend at a campground when that happened.

"I bet her aunt's done it with every guy in town," Chad chimes.

Maybe the bus driver's finally gonna say something this time? Yeah right. Hilda never notices stuff. She's a hater of kids who keeps all her focus on the road. With that squarish face of hers, swallowed by mirrored shades, and lips as thin as rubber bands and always drawn in a sneer, I have to wonder if she'd been carved from a bar

8

of soap instead of brought into the world by parents.

Something brushes my ear. I realize, as it bounces off my guitar case, that it's a blob of bubblegum. Shit bags.

The bus pulls up in front of Chatswick, a four-story brownstone that looks more like a jail than a high school, except for the pig-shaped weathervane, perched on the roof and always pointing south. I scramble off the bus before anyone can see that I'm starting to bawl like a baby.

In the girl's room, I rate the damage. My hair looks like the underside of a school desk. Three hunks of gum cling to the tips of my dirty-blonde strands. Picking these out is easy enough, but getting at the blob of rubber cement in the center of my head, is impossible.

Tammy and Trish, two seniors who always stink of Aqua Net and who share a butt in the last stall every morning, drop F-bombs between toilet flushes. They sound like hens, clucking about who got laid by who or who got knocked up over the summer. Their jangling voices bounce off the tiled walls.

Tammy—who, according to my best friend, Mary, got so pitifully drunk, she let every guy bang her at a kegger once—ignores me while Trish, her eyes lined heavily with blue mascara, shoots me a hard glare from the doorway of the stall as if trying to decide whether or not to kick my ass today. I glare back. The bell for first period rings.

"Freak." Trish nudges me as she and Tammy shuffle past.

I continue the struggle with my hair, then give up. I slip out of the Girl's room and out the glass double-doors, near the school's rear exit and toward the edge of the school's grounds, all of it twinkling with October frost. The morning sun burns my eyes. I squint into the crisp, blue air, then raise my thumb to the oncoming cars.

****

At home, I give it another go, using a jar of Skippy. I've heard somewhere that peanut butter's good for getting stuff out of your hair. When this fails, I try good old Head & Shoulders. The phone rings. I ignore it. It's the school wanting to know why I'm out again.

When the shampoo fails, I try brushing the rubber cement out, using my aunt's barber comb, but the rubber cement has hardened into a frozen, rubbery lump. So, I cut the lump out with my aunt's hairdressing scissors. From my reflection in the cracked mirror, I can see the gap where a good chunk of my hair used to be. I toss the scissors into the water-stained sink.

I blast Joy Division on my turn table and begin jamming along to "Transmission" with my acoustic, putting on a wild concert for my stuffed animals, piled up on the rainbow-patterned comforter in my bedroom. Deepening my voice to sound like Ian Curtis, I croon to the giraffe, but his black button gaze meets mine in the mirror and I realize how stupid I look. I'll never be cool.

Billy, one among many of my aunt's ex-boy-friends—the only one I liked—taught me to play guitar. I was eleven when he and my aunt, who I call Elaine, met at a bowling alley where she used to wait tables. Billy was from Southern California and worked at a boron mine. He liked to move around a lot. Elaine locked eyes on him because he looked like Brian May from the band Queen and claimed to have jammed with Frank Zappa once.

Billy would take Elaine and me to concerts. One Fourth of July we saw the Steve Miller Band, and Elaine'd gotten so wasted, she puked on her shoes and we had to leave during "Fly Like an Eagle." Still, it'd been fun, us hanging out on the grass among all those people, Billy smoking pot and me lighting sparklers.

Billy bought me the acoustic: a factory-made Yamaha. After we'd opened our presents, he sat me down and taught me how to play "Smoke on the Water." That was the Christmas of '77—the best one I'd ever had because it felt like we were a family: Elaine, Billy and me.

They split up on New Year's Eve. Elaine'd screamed, 'Don't you touch me!' when Billy'd tried to hold her. I'd been right there in the living room and didn't see anything wrong in the way he was acting, but Elaine was looking at Billy like she'd seen a ghost, like Billy was this monster who'd invaded our home instead of being this loving, caring boyfriend who'd been helping us get by.

That night was my last memory of Billy. I'd run out into the snow, out in the middle of Dwight Street. It was late. I was wearing just my nightgown and slippers, screaming for him to come back, snot rolling over my lip as I bawled my stupid head off, watching the tail lights of his Dodge Van disappear into the night, blotted out by heavy snow flakes zig zagging out of the sky. When I returned, Elaine was on the living room rug in a fetal position, an empty gaze filling her eyes. I'd never hated her more than I hated her in that moment. I wanted to kick her...but I also wanted to comfort her. Never had I felt so mixed up and so scared, seeing her like that. We never heard from Billy again.

****

It's ten p.m. and I'm starving, but all we have is Skippy Peanut Butter and fish heads. Chuck, Elaine's current flavor of the past three months—a record for her—is saving the fish heads for a chowder he plans to make. Christ, every time I open that fridge, which smells like river bottom, I want to gag from the sight of those fish heads, which I swear are undressing me with their dead jelly eyes.

'Humans've lost touch on how to live off the land,' Chuck told me yesterday, when he came tromping in, wearing rubber knee-highs, beaming with pride as he showed me his slimy, scaly trout, their tails slapping the sides of the pail. 'Why blow money on 'em when you can catch your own?'

Elaine and Chuck had only known each other for a week when she asked him to move in. With Elaine and me living here, the trailer is already cramped. Add Chuck and his pet Boa constrictors, Lenny and Squiggy—named after the two greaser characters from *Lavern and Shirley*—and it's claustrophobic. The trailer smells of snake poop and stale beer and everybody's always on top of each other. I can't pick a wedgie without accidentally elbowing Chuck and I can't ask Elaine private 'girl questions' without Chuck overhearing them through the flimsy walls.

She met him at the Monkey Wrench, the only hot spot in Beckett where she tends bar. She'd been working the closing shift when Chuck got up to sing "Blue Suede Shoes" with a cover band. Elaine is an Elvis nut and Chuck is a sucker for red-haired women. The two instantly hit it off.

Chuck really does sound exactly like Elvis, which is kind of cool, but he's a drunk and he looks like Fred Flintstone with his perpetual five o'clock shadow and caveman's feet: fat and squarish— he's always walking around barefoot. He used to work as a professional clown in psych wards, but because of knee trouble, he now collects disability.

****

At eleven, I light a Winston and flop down on the sagging brown couch that always stinks of Chuck's beer farts, the coils in its cushions poking me no matter which way I sit. Smoke snakes its way up Elaine's blue lampshade with a mermaid pattern. It is one in a set of two she got at a tag sale for two bucks. According to her they're 'vintage, from the sixties, and absolutely gorgeous.' To me, they're something you'd see in a whorehouse. They look dumb among her artwork: mostly of rock celebrities, painted in acrylics.

My favorite painting of hers—not of a rock celebrity— is or *was* one of a naked girl with wide, lidless eyes and no mouth, nude and silhouetted against a red, swirling background, a magazine cut-out of a fetus planted in the center of her belly. The fetus' eyes had looked bulbous and alien-like. Elaine'd had this eager, kid-like look on her face when she'd shown it to me, but I didn't know what to say. The painting creeped me out. It was like the work of a fourth grader—two dimensional and all—but it had something special about it. A mood. A feeling. Elaine's hands were shaky as she'd held it up for me to see. They shook even more when I didn't say much. She shoved the painting back in her bedroom closet, hurt all over her face, and slammed the door. I never saw it again.

A few days later, I snooped through her closet, wanting another look at that painting, but it was gone. After that, she painted a lot less. Her practice in art became, instead, a practice in pouring beer and mixed drinks

****

Flashback Fridays are the busiest at the Monkey Wrench Saloon. Elaine'd talked her boss, Hal, into letting her have Flashback Fridays free, even though they're the big money making nights, so she can watch the Far Out Frankies perform sixties and seventies covers. I guess "California Dreaming," by the Mamas and the Papas, is more important than paying the electric bill—last month the lights went out while I was doing my homework in algebra.

The smell of beer and cigarettes choke the air as I weave my way through the low-ceilinged tavern, lit by Chinese lanterns. Elaine is sitting on her favorite stool, silver and vinyl and in the shape of a giant wrench. John Hanlon, a regular, is sitting on his favorite stool, a cow-printed bucket seat. The two are hanging all over each other. A sea sick feeling fills my stomach with the idea of John becoming her next squeeze.

"Gina, honey!" Elaine slurs when I tap her shoulder. "Hey, ever'body! This my lil niece." She hooks an arm around my waist—her grasp clumsy yet iron-like. She introduces me to her friends even though I know them all. John salutes me with his can of Stroh's. His fingernails are filthy.

"She don't love her auntie no more!" Elaine pouts when I pry myself from her.

"Hi, Gina!" says Sharon, fourteen years Elaine's junior, she has the worst split ends known to mankind.

"Hi," I grunt, my eyes glued on Elaine. "There's no food."

"Don't start." Elaine blows smoke in my face.

"There's no food in the house."

"So whatta ya saying?" Elaine shoves her glass

away.

"There's nothing to eat."

"You accusin' me of bein' a lousy provider?" She claps a hand over her chest. Her lips start to tremble. She leans into Sharon, "My niece is accusin' me of bein' a lousy provider...."

Sharon looks away, suddenly embarrassed for Elaine as she pretends to be interested in the Far Out Frankies. John tosses me a snaky grin, beer foam caught in his mustache. I glare at him while Elaine dumps bills from her purse—tip money from a long day's work—onto the bar. A quarter bounces away. A five-dollar bill flutters to the floor. I stuff it into my jean's pocket while Elaine, not so nimble, takes a painstaking effort to sort and smooth out the other bills, separating the ones from the fives.

"Here, Elaine," I groan, trying to lump it into one stack. "Put it away before you—"

"I know! " She slaps my hand while Hal, the only guy I know who can pull off a ZZ Top beard without looking dumb, flashes me a pitying smile from behind the bar.

"I'm just trying to—"

"Leave me alone. Go get yourself something to eat." Elaine tosses me a few bucks, the hurt never leaving her face.

"Are you hungry? Want me to get you something?"

She ignores me and orders another drink.

****

The I.G.A., down the road, is closed. I missed it by five minutes. I return to the Monkey Wrench, but the kitchen'd stopped serving. Hal asks one of the help to throw a sandwich together for me.

The dance floor fills quickly when the band plays "Family Affair" by Sly & the Family Stone. Two women with feathered hair and jeans so tight they've got camel toe, do a dance called The Bump. One loses her balance and falls into the lap of a guy wearing a Bart's Auto and Wrecking baseball cap. The puffy sleeves on Elaine's dress have slipped off her shoulders. She is bawling into John's shirt front. Her mascara is running in thick, black streaks. Her long hair, the color of an Irish Setter, hangs in her face. Why she is crying, I don't know.

"Finish your drink. Let's go," I tell her after pushing my plate away.

"Who're you, Jiminy Cricket?" John laughs. His teeth are brown and pitted.

"No, no...Gina's right." Elaine peels herself from John.

"Give me your keys, Elaine."

"Lemme go to the little girl's room." She sniffles, her movements clumsy as she takes the wad of bar napkins from me.

"I'll give you gals a ride," John says with a dirty twinkle in his good eye. His glass eye gazes at nothing, like the eyes of Chuck's fish heads. He'd had it put in a year ago, after his hunting accident.

"We don't want a ride." I say, then look to

Elaine. "I'll grab your coat while you pee. Meet me at the door."

****

Fifteen minutes pass. She's not at the door. She's not in any of the toilet stalls, one of which she'd been known to pass out in. She's back at the bar with another drink.

"Come off it, Elaine! I wanna go home!" I yell in her face, throwing her cheetah-print coat at her.

"Then go home, Gina." She lets the jacket fall to the floor.

"You're being an idiot!"

"Yeah? I'm not the one making a scene."

I kick the coat. She kicks it back. The camel-toed women, who'd been dancing the bump, step over the coat to get to the bar. They shoot Elaine a dirty look.

"This is the second time this week—fix your dress, Elaine! You look like a slut!"

The regulars ignore us while the two women stare at us. I could care less. Elaine and me are already legend-ary in the tiny town of Beckett.

"God! God! God! Leave me *alone*. Why do ya gotta be so *mean* to me?" Elaine slams her empty glass on the bar. She's crying again. "See this, Hal? See how mean she is to me?"

"Go home, Elaine. You're shut off anyway."

Sharon and Hal drag my aunt, helpless at this point, to the car.

"Gina, I'm sober enough. Let me get you guys home."

Sharon tries to take Elaine's keys from me, even though her breath is more fermented than Elaine's.

"No thanks." I slip into the driver's seat of Elaine's brown Cutlass, which I jokingly call 'the Gutless.' It stinks of ashtray. Foam stuff leaks from the cracks in its vinyl seats.

The Gutless wheezes when I crank the key before spluttering to a grumbling idle. I got my permit a week ago, which allows me to legally do what I've been doing for the last year and a half: chauffeur Elaine.

We do twenty-five all the way home, Elaine singing, "Blood'sss thicker than the mud...come on, Gina, ssing. Sssing with me. Iss a family affair...Isss a family affair...Iss a family affair...s' a family affair...."

****

Back at the trailer, I let Elaine make her own damn way up the wobbly steps by beating her to the bathroom. Over the flushing of the toilet, I can hear her thump up the hall. Here we go.

"Don't you ever pull that shit again, like you did tonight!" She yells in my face as I'm brushing my teeth. I spit in the sink.

"Look at me when I'm talkin' to you!" Elaine blocks me from getting to the faucet. Our bathroom is tiny, but with the two of us it's impossible.

"Go to bed, Elaine." I reach around her to run the faucet.

"What's all the commotion?" Chuck's bulk fills the doorway. His hairy gut quakes over the waistband of his Fruit of the Looms and is truly amazing to watch. It moves independently from the rest of him when he talks. Standing half-naked like that, he reminds me of this weird sea creature I'd seen on Nova once—some kind of Manatee, I think. Whatever it was, it mated with the girl Manatee....The idea of Chuck and Elaine getting it on turns my stomach.

"What're you gals hollerin' about now?" Chuck picks his underwear out of his butt.

"I've got school tomorrow. You deal with her." I push past him. Elaine follows me up the hall, screaming as she teeters into the wall, plastered with framed rock band photos. An autographed one of Peter Frampton, her favorite, lands with a bang and shatters. Chuck shrugs, like he always does and returns to the bedroom.

"You spoiled my evening, you blight. You shoulda never been born!"

"Right back at ya, *Auntie* Elaine." I kick open my bedroom door, knowing how much she hates it when I call her that.

"Get outta my face!"

"I'm not in your face. You're in mine." I slam the door.

It's funny how she yells at me to go away, when what she really wants is for me to stand there so she'll have someone to fight with. Chuck's no fun. He's about as bland as a boiled hotdog. He never offers an opinion of his own. Elaine and me have had worse tiffs, but the best trick in ending them is if I shut my door and push my chair under the knob.

"Go to bed!" Elaine shrieks and the chair rattles against the flimsy door.

I wonder, as I hit the lights, if Ms. Keets'll call the cops again. A tiny plot of grass divides her trailer from ours, so not much escapes her ears. Sunrise Trailer Park is made up of fifteen mobile homes, all huddled in a tight cluster, on an island in the middle of the murky Piska River. The river banks are cluttered with electric towers. There's an abandoned paper mill on one side and a waste water treatment plant on the other. Most everyone else in Beckett lives in those old, white farm houses among the rolling, wooded hills. Wish Elaine and me lived in one of those. Mary, my best friend, lives in one of those—a renovated one with a view of the valley.

Elaine gives up sooner than usual. Guess she doesn't have much fire in her tonight. But I know, just know that I won't be getting any sleep tonight. It's always the same.

****

I gaze at myself in Elaine's makeup mirror, now suctioned to the refrigerator. With great care, I run the hairdressing scissors along the edge of the salad bowl, which I'd placed on my head as soon as I felt awake enough to deal with my hair situation.

Elaine's been holed up in the bathroom for over an hour, retching. She shuffles her way to the kitchen, in her robe, as I'm sweeping the tufts of hair off the linoleum floor.

"Why didn't you tell me we were out of food, Gina?" She stares into the open fridge for a long time, something she'd yell at me for doing, then grabs a beer.

I roll my eyes. "You remember what you said to me last night?"

"No." Her face is the color of a green potato chip. Her hands tremble as she chases four Tylenol with a can of Schlitz. She glances at my hair—now quite short—from the corner of her eye, and nearly chokes. "What'd you do to your hair?"

"Looks like crap, doesn't it?" I jerk away when she tries to touch it. I pour myself coffee and light a cigarette.

She shrugs, looking away. She clutches the edge of the kitchen table as she sits, as if doing so'll keep her from spinning off the edge of the globe. The table is cluttered with empty beer cans, cut up coupons and overdue bills. She never sorts through her junk.

"Will you take me to the salon to have it fixed?" I never like for her to cut my hair.

"Can't afford it, babe." She looks away, taking another pull from her Schlitz.

"Great. What the fuck am I supposed to do?"

"Gina, don't swear—"

"This is so not fair!"

"Lower your voice." She drops her head in her palm.

I slam my mug down in the sink and storm to the living room, the whole trailer shaking from my footsteps. I throw myself down on the couch to sulk. Elaine gets up to follow, a smoke trail coiling around her scrawny frame like a snake squeezing the life of its prey. She drags hard on her cigarette. Exhales.

"Gina?"

"What?"

"It's not the end of the world. Hair grows back."

She doesn't get it. I'm already the laughing stock at Chatswick. She may only be thirty-one-years-old and younger than mothers of girls my age, but when it comes to her ability to 'get me' it's like she's like a million-years-old or something.

"I'll fix your hair."

Great.

I hold very still in the straight-backed chair while Elaine, a Newport dangling from her mouth, works the scissors along my neck. With her hangover shakes, I'm scared she'll slip and cut me, and that I'll bleed like Chuck does when he nicks himself shaving. The wisps and ringlets pool around her slippers. I start to wonder how much she plans to chop as the cool air brushes my neck.

She finishes. I head for the mirror. Holding my breath, I hit the bathroom switch.

"Not bad, eh?" Elaine stands behind me with her hands on her hips as tears sting my eyes.

"I look like Rod Stewart."

She laughs.

"It's not funny!"

"Relax. You don't look like Rod Stewart."

"You're right. I look like David Bowie, actually, which would be cool if I were a guy!"

"Hey, man, that style used to be the cutting

edge—"

"*Used* to be—"

"They called it a shag—"

"Great, Elaine. Nobody in school has hair like this? You know how long it took me to get it to the middle of my back? To feather it like...like—"

"Who? The Charlie's Angels?" She makes a gagging gesture. "Gina, you don't wanna look like a bimbo. Trust me."

"No, but I didn't wanna look like a guy—"

"Throw some makeup on, then." She tosses her makeup bag on the counter. "Don't know what else to tell you. You're the one who chopped your hair off." She storms out.

The purple eyeliner looks cool, but I don't know what I'm supposed to do with the pencil, and worry I'll poke my eye out with it. At fifteen, I feel dumb asking for help since everyone I know started wearing the stuff by the time they were thirteen—but I associate makeup with being a slut. I always know when Elaine's about to go on one of her manhunts, by how much of that crap she loads on her face.

She returns with a tiny, velvet box. "This belonged to your mother. I was planning to give it to you for your six-teenth but..." Elaine holds up a delicate, gold chain with a tiny, blue stone. It shimmers in the overhead lighting. "It's your December birthstone."

At least this time she's giving me something decent and not something creepy. Her last 'I'm sorry for last night' present had been a magenta-colored teddy with matching panties—a regift from her ex, who she'd met at a salon where she used to cut hair. She'd fallen for Bruce because he looked like Jimmy Page, only he wasn't a musician, he pumped gas. We moved in with him when I was twelve, into his motel room, until he went to jail for a long time. The reason is still a mystery because Elaine tells me nothing.

"Thanks," I mumble as she clasps the chain around my neck, her hands shaking like crazy. It's nice and all, but it doesn't make up for last night.

She gazes at the two of us together in the mirror—her reflection on the right side of the crack, mine on the left—with that hurt look, the same hurt look she'd had the day she'd shown me her painting, yet a bit haunted like it was after she threw Billy out. It's giving me the creeps.

Me and Elaine look a lot alike. Our bodies are thin and built like a rope. Our skin is the color of bleached sand dollars, delicate and breakable, our cheeks smattered with freckles. Our eyes are moss green, other times blue, depending on what color shirt we wear. But our hair is different—and so are our chins. Hers is small and perfect. Mine has a deep cleft that looks like a deer's paw print. It's my least favorite feature, aside from my gray tooth and the caterpillar scar on my elbow—from the time I fell off my skateboard.

According to the one photo Elaine'd given me of my father—which I carry in my bag—I got my dirty-blonde hair from him. All I know about him is that his name is Roger, that he was my mother's high school sweetheart, and that he doesn't have a cleft. For years I've wondered who else in the family has one, but Elaine tells me never to annoy her with questions, not even ones about my grandparents, whom I've never met—and she never, ever, wants me talking about Roger. And all I know about my mother is that her name was Ellen and that she and Elaine were identical twins, and that they'd grown up in Queens. I'd like to go there someday, just to see where Elaine and Ellen grew up, just to know something, anything about my background. Besides, Juilliard's down there too, and I've always wanted to see Juilliard, and to be like those kids on *Fame*.

'They got lost in a house fire,' Elaine told me once when I asked for photos of Ellen. It's like the woman never existed.

"Don't worry about your hair. It doesn't look that bad." Elaine looks ready to cry.

She gets that way sometimes and I don't know why. But what can I do? She never tells me what's on her mind.

****

"Hey, Gina. Dig the hair!" Barb laughs when I board the bus with my guitar.

"What happened to her hair?" says Kelly, who everyone calls Belly Kelly because she's pregnant.

"Bet she had to cut the gum out," Chaz says.

"Nah, I think she turned dyke on us. A dyke who thinks she's Nancy Wilson with the guitar," Barb hisses.

I keep my eyes glued on the scenery flashing past,

clutching the music books I'd checked out at the library: *America's Jazz Artists* and *So, You Want to Be in a Rock Band: a Beginner's Guide to Performing in Public.*

"Gina and Missy Mayfield have something going on between 'em," Barb clucks.

Missy Mayfield, known as the Bearded Lady at school, is another one of Chatswick's underdogs. She and I are in Phys. Ed. together and are always the last ones picked for dodgeball. She's okay, I guess, kind of quiet. Then again, so am I.

"Isn't it true that they lezz out in the equipment room?"

"I'm gonna shove those eyes so far into your head they're gonna look like two pissholes in a snow bank!" I wheel around to face Chaz, who suddenly looks terrified.

"Ooooh, hostility!" Surprise flickers in Barb's eyes.

I hate her eyes. Before I knew what she was like, I thought they were this pretty, slate gray color. Now, they just look like the color of dirty dishwater. Her turned up nose looks witchy to me.

"Ooooh, what're ya—"

"Young lady in the back..." Hilda glances in her rearview—a first—the highway reflecting in her mirrored shades. "Shut your trap or I'll write you up."

Silence. The only sound on the bus is the hum of the engine and the sigh of oncoming traffic. Chaz suddenly erupts in his nervous, hyena laugh and everyone else snickers, except for Barb, whose face burns red, her eyes simmering with hate as she glares at me. I grin back. Fuck you, Barb.

****

"Missing nine days in one month is not good, Miss Laramee. If you do the math, that's more than two days of school missed each week," says Mr. Fisher, who everyone at Chatswick calls 'Big Fish,' as he mops the sweat from his thinning hair with a hankie.

The flesh of his big belly squeezes between the buttons of his wide-lapeled shirt. It presses against his heavy oak desk, empty but for his black attendance book with Fall 1982 stamped in gold lettering, and a really crummy photo of two homely little boys. I'm guessing they're his. One boy has eyes red as a rat's from staring into the camera. The other has a finger lodged up his nose. Does Big Fish lecture them the way he does his students? 'Wetting the bed nine nights in one month is not good, Johnny. If you do the math, that's....'

"Something funny?"

I didn't know I was smirking until Big Fish called me on it. The chair I sit in is one of those fake leather ones with brass rivets that go across the back. I wish it would swallow me up. The sun streaming in the window reflects on Big Fish's desk and in the lenses of his chunky glasses. Unable to see his eyes, it's hard know what he's thinking. He flips through my file. The clock ticking over the door seems way too loud, so does his breathing.

"You barely passed freshman year."

I want to remind him that I got As in music and art.

"Your apathy is not conducive to the learning environment, Miss Laramee." He starts to wheeze. "I don't know why you bother coming to school."

"I don't cause trouble. I'm not even rude to the teachers...not like some of the kids are."

He toots from his inhaler, coughs once. "You've chosen to fail quietly and I appreciate that, but to play an active role in society, participation and a good attitude starts within the high school walls...."

He should've been a shrink.

"So, I'm contacting Ms. Elaine Laramee so we may have a meeting between the three of us."

****

"Damn it, Gina," Elaine sighs when I drop by the Wrench to tell her about my trip to Big Fish's, thinking it'll soften the blow for when she gets the phone call.

She grabs two Michelob mugs, dips them in the tiny sink filled with sanitizer, before lining them neatly on the terri-cloth towel. She repeats the routine with two tumblers. A long strand of hair, having escaped her ribbon barrette, curves gently around her freckled cheek. Her mid-riff tank-top shows off her flat stomach—as well as her cleavage when she leans over. This draws the attention of James, another Monkey Wrench pervert who, up until then'd been watching golf on the TV, mounted above a row of gin bottles.

James has spidery veins that explode across his knob-like nose and no neck. He's one of Elaine's favorites because he tips her big. He refers to her as 'the Monkey Wench.' She finds this endearing, I find it degrading.

James reminds me of Teddy, the self-proclaimed inventor who came into our lives when I was thirteen. Teddy had Elaine convinced he was independently wealthy. Really, he was a con man with a gambling problem. He stole all her money and we got evicted from our studio. Elaine's ex-friend, Ruthie, rescued us by lending Elaine money to get into Sunrise Trailer Park, which Elaine never paid back.

"When're you gonna stop screwing up, Gina?" Elaine rings up James. "I'm trying, I really am...busting my hump, trying to put food—"

"There's no food in the house." I slouch on the bar stool, then stiffen when John lurches out of the men's room, letting out a belch as he zips his fly.

"You'll know what going hungry is if I have to take time off work to deal with the noise at school, and don't get smart with me...and stop stealing my cigarettes." She gives me a dirty look when I take a Newport from her pack.

"I ran out."

"Should get you an after school job, kid." John stands a tad too close to me as he runs a greasy thumbnail across a scratch ticket. He fixes cars for a living, which is why his hands are always filthy.

"Sheeitt. Didn' fuckin' win nothin'." He tosses the ticket onto the bar.

"Gina," Elaine reaches into her tip jar. "While you're buying cigarettes, get us something to eat at the I.G.A., will ya?"

"Sure."

"Have supper ready. I'll be home at ten."

"Will you?"

"What do you mean, will I? If I say I'll be home at ten, I'll be home at ten—"

"Elaine, baby, get me another round," John- says.

"Go on, Gina. I'm working." Her bracelets make a tinkling sound as she shoos me away.

I glance over my shoulder. James is still gawk- ing at Elaine's cleavage. She's leaning over the bar, letting Dottie, another regular who claims to have psychic powers, read her palm.

John gawks at Elaine's ass, which I admit does look great in those stone-washed jeans of hers. She barely notices John and James, and is smiling sadly at Dottie, as if Dottie's telling her something she'd rather not hear.

I try to eavesdrop, but it's hard to hear over the bleeping of a Pac-Man game. Scott, the dishwash- er, sits slumped near the door, playing probably his tenth round. He can't get enough of it.

A yellow flyer taped to the door, catches my eye as I'm leaving. Five bands are scheduled to play tomorrow night, including the Suzi Bowman Band—my favorite. I snag the flyer and step out. I toss another glance back at Elaine. James is stuffing money in her bra. She's laughing as she smacks James on the shoulder. John just ogles her like a panting, dirty dog.

****

A rumbling sound startles me awake. The TV'd lost its reception. The trailer is filled with white noise. I'd been watching *Fame*—I never miss an episode—while waiting for Elaine and must've fallen asleep.

My pulse slows when I recognize the sound of the Cutlass rolling into the driveway. The glare from its head-lights creeps through the plastic blinds. Shadows, looking like prison bars, stretch across the low ceiling. It's 3:00 a.m.

The door bangs open. Elaine wipes her feet on the mat with vigor, looking like a bull ready to charge. Her hair is mussed like she'd been rolling around in the woods. I follow her to the kitchen. She flops down in the chair, lights a Newport, then props her feet on the table—something she'd yell at me for doing.

"Gina, honey, you shoulda seen the band that played tonight at the Wrench." Booze wafts from her breath as she exhales smoke. "The drummer, ooh la la. Sharon had to pry me offa him...I mean he looked just like Gregg Allman from the Allman Brothers...and he uh...what's his name...? Right. *Dag*. Short for Dagger. He calls himself Dagger 'cause he has an extensive knife collection. He showed it to me...Sharon and I went to his pad and I got to ride on the back of his Harley...it's why I'm late gettin' in.

"Was gonna have my way with him but Sharon

dragged me away before we could get our trunks down." Elaine giggles. "Got his number, though. Told him all about you. He wants to meet you."

"Great, Elaine. What about Chuck?"

She scrunches her nose as if I've spoken to her in Japanese. "What about him? He's at Buddy's. Anyway, I ought to kick his lazy ass out 'long with those fuckin' snakes." She thrusts a boney finger at Lenny and Squiggy, asleep in their cage near the heater. "Damn things eat better 'n we do, especially Squiggy."

True. The monster is six-feet-long and fat around as my bicep. But I'm fascinated by him. I enjoy watching him choke the life out of the rats Chuck feeds him. The blood squirting the sides of the tank is quite something, but watching the rats get swallowed whole is even better. They'll then become a shapeless lump inside Squiggy's tube-like body. They'll sit there for what seems like forever. I've always wondered, judging by a snake's anatomy, how it is they take a shit. I'll have to ask Chuck sometime.

"Dag and I talked about the three of us getting together. If it works out, I want you to look your best. I've got this sexy halter you can wear. It's pastel pink. It'll go beautifully with your skin, and you're *gonna* wear makeup."

"Elaine, what're you talking about?" I glare at her through sleep-logged eyes.

"Can't have my niece looking like a twelve-year-old tomboy who puts no thought into her appearance." She sneers at the patch stitched on the crotch of my jeans, which I've worn for four days in a row.

"It's three in the morning. You're drunk. Go to bed."

"You're such a prig, Gina. How it is we came from the same gene pool is beyond me." She opens the fridge. "Have a beer."

"I don't want that." I wave a hand when she offers me a Schlitz.

"What's for supper?" she asks as I yank the oven door. It squeals in protest before falling open with a clatter.

"What in Christ is that?" She sneers at the slice of Stouffer's french bread pizza, clinging in one greasy mass to the wire rack. It resembles the dead squirrel at the end of our driveway.

"Dinner that was ready five fucking hours ago."

"You aren't too old to have your mouth washed out with soap."

"Well, you shouldn't've gone to that guy's house." I hand her the plate with an accusing eye.

She looks at me funny, panic in her eyes, like she's seeing something, a ghost maybe, but I'm too pissed off to care.

"It's your fault—"

Elaine shoves me. I stumble, the plate hits the floor. My eyes bug. She's always been a yeller, but this is the first time she's been violent.

"Get out!"

"Elaine—"

"I'm done with you—flunking school, disrupting the class, and now disrespecting me. Think it's a joy ride?

Trying to make ends meet for the both of us—
tending bar? I didn't have to keep you—"

"*Keep* me?"

Elaine turns her back. She swigs from her beer.
"I didn't have to take you in—"

"Then why did you? No one told you to. You're
acting like a victim!"

"Because I am...." Her voice drops to a whisper.
She shakes her head, slams her beer down. "Stay
away from the men, Gina...."

Ridiculous. Number one, I'm a virgin. Two, I've
never even been kissed. Three, no guy—except
for this kid named Calvin with his caterpillar-look-
ing eyebrows—in his right mind would ask me on
a date. If she was more involved with my life, she'd
have no reason to panic when it comes to sex.

"Never go around asking for it, Gina."

"Asking for what? You're the one who told me
to dress like a slut for some dude you barely met."

"I'm still paying dearly for Ellen's choices."

The 'Ellen rant' comes during her worst drunks.
See, Ellen being unmarried and getting knocked
up at sixteen was inexcusable in their dad's eyes.
She was told to move out. Roger, the boy in that
photo I carry, accused her of cheating on him.
Ellen moved into a friend's, gave birth, then fled
to Manhattan, leaving me with Elaine. A month
later, Elaine got exactly one phone call from Ellen,
letting her know she was okay but that she wasn't
coming back—she was busy making a film with
Edie Sedgwick. Dead? Alive? Elaine doesn't know,

but moving upstate was her way of rescuing me from New York City's grip, so that I wouldn't end up like Ellen.

"Gina, you don't wanna be pregnant and sleeping on someone's couch—"

"This is getting old—"

"What's all the commotion?" Chuck lumbers in, his jacket smelling like campfire. "I could hear you gals from the end of the driveway."

"Stay out of it, Charles—"

"D'you get rid of that dead squirrel like you promised?" I ask. Chuck belches, shrugs and slinks off to the bedroom.

Loser.

"I'm still picking up the pieces."

"Elaine, you're making me feel like I'm a mistake—"

"You don't understand—"

"I heard you."

"Why bother talking?"

"You hurt me when you talk like that—"

"Clean this up and go to bed, Gina." She tosses a rag to the floor, spattered with pizza sauce and begins sifting through her extensive record collection.

"Monday Morning" drifts from the living room turn table. She always plays the Mamas and the Papas whenever she's feeling bummed out. I can hear her crying all the way down the hall as I hide in my closet with my guitar.

****

I open my locker and find streamers of used toilet

paper dangling off the coat hook. I clap a hand over my nose to keep from gagging. Todd, from my English class, has a locker next to mine. He shoots me a filthy look as he grabs his text.

"Whew! Someone shit their pants?" Bobby Pierce's voice echoes up the hall.

"Gina Laramee forgot to shower today." Barb's voice floats behind me as I stand frozen, gazing dumbly at my algebra text. It's in the back of the locker but I can't grab it without my arm brushing against the toilet paper.

"Gross," Kara chimes.

Mrs. Larson, the English teacher, steps into the hall. She cranes her skinny neck, flecked with fleshy moles, the kind that are so big I want to snip them off with a pair of pruners. She furrows her brow, then wrinkles her nose, eyeing Barb and Kara with suspicion. The two are snorting behind their books. Barb mutters, "Gina's aunt's a slut!" under her breath as they waddle past.

"Gina, where are you going?" Mrs. Larson calls in a pleading voice as I run for the red, neon EXIT sign, the tears coming before I even reach the glass, double doors.

****

In Chatswick's student lot, I lounge on the hood of Mary's yellow Corvette, watching the cheerleaders leave the gym. There's a bounce in their step that causes their perky little jugs to vibrate under the nylon of their gold jerseys. Black and gold pompoms spill over the tops of knapsacks. Clean shaven, popsicle stick-legs flash from the hems of black miniskirts. They look like a bee colony.

Barb, queen of the bees, is the last to leave. She walks with a swish of her hips, casually tossing her ponytail over her shoulder. My heart races when she falls in step with Mary and the two walk elbow to elbow, their pace slowing as they chat.

I ground my cigarette into the blacktop. When I look up Mary is walking away from Barb and trotting in my direction, her dark, chestnut waves shaking loose from her ribbon barrettes. Barb hangs back, shooting me a nasty grin. Mary's head is bowed against the wind. She doesn't see me flip Barb the bird.

"What're you doing here?" Mary's the only one among the cheerleaders not wearing her uniform. She tosses it on the hood of the Corvette. With her big, dark eyes and perfect skin she could pass for a model in *Seventeen*, except for that gap between her front teeth.

"You're never here past three o'clock unless you're in detention," she giggles. "Listen, I can't wait to tell you something—"

"You're never at the house anymore. I didn't know what else to do." I've been hanging out with her mom more than her.

A week ago, Mrs. Blum and I hung out on the couch, me watching General Hospital, her crocheting a dog sweater for Boss, their poodle. "She's got a boyfriend, Gina. I'm sure of it. She hasn't brought him to the house so Father and I can meet him...and she's never around for supper anymore. I tried hunting her down at all her hangouts, even Happy Fridays...."

Happy Fridays, a run down roller rink and burger joint, on the edge of Beckett, is one of the few places in Washburn County that'll put up with kids. You have to have a car to get there, but it's the favored hang out of Barb and Kara's. I avoid the place the way one might avoid a lover with Syphilis.

"I'm not avoiding you, Gina...you know you could invite me to your house once in a while."

The first—and last time—I invited Mary to my place, Elaine, half in the bag on Rum and Cokes, pranced out to the living room in just her skimpy tie-dye nighty and began showing Mary her zoo-rock collection before Mary could even get her jacket off.

Elaine's zoo rocks are made up of smooth river stones, about the size of a softball. She'd collect these along the river banks and then hand paint them. One among her collection has zebra stripes, another has leopard spots, all have whiskers made of pipe cleaners and tails made of yarn—the rocks weren't the problem. It was her Keith Moon story that pissed me off. She bragged to Mary about having flashed her tits at one of the roadies, at a Who concert, in order to get backstage so she could get Keith Moon's autograph.

"Oh, she's alright, Gina. At least she gives you your space—"

"Can you come out and see music with me

tonight?"

"I don't know, Gina. Ma's still pissed at me." Mary unlocks the passenger door. "But, hey, you won't believe what I did—"

"It's Friday night. You don't have school. Tell her we're going to the movies. She lets you see movies, right?"

Mary smiles limply, unlocking the driver's door. It's an oven inside, even though it's been one of those crisp, mid-October days because the seats are made of black leather. They smell like cigarettes and jasmine oil. The '75 Corvette Coupe belongs to Mary's dad, but it'll be hers by summer time if she pulls straight As.

"I was fifteen minutes late getting in last night." Mary smiles, turning the key. The rumble of the engine nearly drowns out our voices. "Which, by the way, I have to tell you—"

"Who does she expect you to be, Mary Ingalls from *Little House on the Prairie* or Mary Blum from the year 1982?" I wrinkle my nose.

"Eleven o'clock's my curfew. What can I do?" Mary furrows her brows while throwing the stick in reverse. The tires make a horrific KA-PLUNK as she runs the corvette into a huge pot hole.

"Am I taking you home?" She lights a cigarette.

"I was hoping not. I met you at school for a reason—"

"That's cool."

"Why don't we hang out at your house?"

"No way."

"Well, where's there to go?"

"We could go for a hike...or have dinner at Happy Fridays—"

"Not Happy Fridays. Let's just drive."

"Sure, Gina." Mary blows perfect smoke rings. I try to copy her, only they come out looking like soggy onion rings.

Mary and me are a couple of hot shits cruising around, blaring REO Speedwagon with our window down, our hair snapping in the breeze. I let my arm dangle freely, then wave to a long-haired boy in a denim jacket, in the crosswalk at the end of the school driveway.

"Ma will ground me again if I'm not careful." Mary's eyes look faraway and dreamy. She stomps the brake in order to avoid hitting the boy who seems oblivious. "I can't afford a whole month without Steve. He'll dump me for an older chick who doesn't have a curfew...who isn't strapped in."

"Come on, Mare. You're not strapped in. You just got your license. What good's it gonna do you if you don't get out and do stuff? Anyway, we'll be back by eleven...it's the Suzi Bowman Band." I nudge her. "You dragged me out to see her when she played last year's homecoming. Remember?"

"I remember."

At the homecoming, I was instantly taken by Suzi's throaty baritone voice and her coal-black hair. I'd never seen a chick play an electric or lead a band—Billy may've gotten me into music but it was Suzi who made me want to be in a band.

"Remember that dude you tried to set me up with? The one that looked like Burt from *Sesame Street* 'cause of his bushy eyebrows that went straight across?"

"Calvin?" Mary pitches her cigarette out the window. "I introduced you to him?" She looks thoughtful. "I guess I did...he was nice, but you barely talked to him."

"He was weird." Annoyance springs out of nowhere as I light another Winston. He tried to shove his tongue in my mouth when we kissed in the bleachers, even though I didn't want him to, and then would call the house like ten times a day. I was sorry I gave him my number.

"I was trying to get you out of your dark little shell—"

"Barb and Michelle Thompson kept yelling, 'dorks go home' at Calvin and me from the bleachers."

"I don't remember that."

"Of course you don't." I exhale smoke from my nose in one billowing jet.

"What's your problem?" Mary pumps the break. She pulls into a Burger King.

"I don't have a problem."

"You're being a bitch for no reason." She parks in front of the playground.

"How can you hang with that crowd and still be friends with me?"

"Barb and I are not that good of friends, Gina. We're in the same circle 'cause we're on the cheerleading team." Mary faces me.

"Where do I fit in, in the grand scheme of things?" I sigh, not looking at Mary. "Why did you become friends with me?"

"Because I fucking like you. Because you're fun— when you're not in one of your downer moods. I can be myself when I'm with you and...I don't know, you're talented. Why do you always need to hear my reasons? Why can't you ever just trust me?"

Because I can't trust anyone and I can't handle my life anymore....

"No one trusts me these days and I've kind of had it," Mary presses her hand to her forehead, "Up to here—"

"Hope something bad happens to Barb. Hope she gets knocked up by some loser." I gaze at a guy and a girl dry humping in the back seat of a red, Pontiac Firebird, parked next to us.

"Geezum crow. I know she isn't particularly nice to you, but why the hostility?" Mary leans on the steering wheel.

"She's a big reason why I'm dropping out of school," My voice shakes.

"Dropping...out?"

The drone of the Corvette's engine drowns out my sobs. Mini rainbows glow from the ends of my eyelashes as teardrops gather at their tips and then fall. The sun, shimmering through the dust-streaked windshield, hurts my eyes. I wish the sun would set—plop itself behind the tree line and not come out until I'm ready for it to.

"Gina?" Mary kills the engine. "Why are you dropping out?"

"The toilet paper in my locker?" My voice sounds nasally and hoarse. Mary looks blank.

"Wow, a story that hasn't reached every ear in Washburn County—"

"Toilet paper in your locker?"

"*Used* toilet paper…never mind."

"When'd you decide you were gonna drop out?"

"Now."

"But...what'll you do if you're not in school?" Mary gapes.

"Work with Elaine."

"At that *bar*?"

"It's a tavern, Mary—"

"You aren't really gonna drop out." Pity and panic fills Mary's voice. She wags her head from side to side.

"Yes, I am."

"You're just upset. Tomorrow you'll feel better—"

"No, Mary. I won't. I won't feel better tomorrow."

"You'll be stuck working in places like this." She nods her chin at a dude, wearing a polyester johnny and Burger King visor that doesn't cover his bald spot. He's sweeping the cigarette butts off the walkway. "You want that?"

"Of course not, Mare. I'm gonna work at the Wrench until I can get up enough money to pick up and—"

"But, I mean, what're you gonna *do*?"

"Play music...go to Juilliard...maybe. You know that school in New York?"

"You need a high school diploma to get into Juilliard."

"Okay. I can't talk about this right now." I lean back and close my eyes.

****

"I care about you, Gina. That's the last time I'll say it. It's up to you to believe it." Mary hands me my Whopper, wrapped in steamy, waxed paper.

I calm myself on a dose of brain freeze, brought on by the chocolate shake and the grease-soaked fries that are so salty I gotta wonder if the potatoes were grown in the Utah Salt Flats.

"Thanks for the food."

"You're welcome, now how'll we sneak into the Monkey Wrench without being seen?" Mary sips a Diet Coke.

"You're coming?"

"Sure. Never been inside the Monkey Wrench. Sounds like it might be fun. Maybe I can get some guy to buy me a drink and you can drive us home," she laughs, knowing I don't drink, but she sure does. With a twenty-four-year-old boyfriend, how could she not?

****

The roof of the Monkey Wrench glows yellow from the light of the harvest moon. The lot is mobbed with souped up Fords, jacked up Chevy Novas—the average, every day shit-box cars. I feel like royalty, rolling into the lot in a corvette, although I'm ready to strangle Mary as she takes an eternity trying to park. I'm even more ready to strangle her as she takes her sweet time applying lip gloss, asking, 'Does my hair look okay? Is my mascara smudged? Can you see the zit on my chin?' The cymbal crashes and thumping bass lines, echoing across the lot, are calling me.

"Think we'll get caught—"

"No, Mary. You've asked me that like ten times."

Exhaust fumes and burning rubber choke the air as people peel in and out of the lot. Two young men guzzle forties in the flatbed of the rusty Datsun, parked next to us.

"Nice ass, babe," one mutters to Mary when we pass. She sneers, walking faster.

"Think you're too good for me?" He says. Mary stiffens, shooting me a nervous look.

"Bitch."

"Ignore him," I tell Mary.

"Think I pass for eighteen?" Mary runs a comb through her hair.

"If you smoke a cigarette and act like you don't give a shit, people'll think you're older. Don't get cold feet on me, Mary."

We slip around the back of the building, then hide behind the dumpster, stinking of garbage and fried food. "Let the Good Times Roll" by The Cars wafts from the kitchen door, clashing with the honky-tonk sounds of The Beaver Bedlam Boys. Mary and I step closer to the door, pressing our noses to the screen.

The zit-faced busboys scurry in and out the swinging doors that connect the kitchen to the tavern, carrying stacks of dirty plates dripping with leftovers. Steam billows from the dish machine, curling lazily in the heavy air, clinging to the yellowed walls, slick and dingy from years of hamburger grease. The dish machine thrums between shouts and the banging of pots as Scott, the dishwasher shoves racks of silverware through.

Manny and Ed, two sweaty cooks, wear chef coats that are so spattered with marinara, they look like mafia victims. They bustle behind the line, trying not to bang into each other. One mans the fryer, the other the grill, piled with ribs and wings.

Manny, the elder with tattoos and pitted skin, works in a calm, orderly way, while Ed heaves sizzlers and monkey dishes in the direction of the sink, spattering poor Scott, who's too short on brain cells—from having, according to Elaine, huffed too many whipped-cream cans—to notice he's being christened with scampi sauce.

"Alli-son!" Ed smacks the bell. DING! DING! "Pick up your fucking order! Fries for table ten are as cold as my dead aunt's tits!"

Allison, wearing a tank top two sizes too small, looks ready to cry. "Be a doll and bring these fries to table ten," she says to Scott.

"We can't go in there," Mary whines, looking horrified.

"No kidding." I step away from the screen.

"Forget it, Gina. Let's just catch a movie." Mary drags her heels when I try the door to the linen room.

"What're you doing?" She hisses when I pull her inside. It stinks of dirty aprons and cleaning supplies. The only light comes from the door frame on the other side of the room.

"We shouldn't be doing this." She stumbles into a pile of linen bags as we inch our way in the dark, toward the door leading to the dried goods storage area.

"Gina...this is dumb." She wipes her hands on her pegged jeans.

"You're always bitching how you can never break away. Well, here's your chance." We enter the storage area. I pull the ball chain and the lights go out. We crouch in the dark, among ten pound cans of tuna and boxes of Kosher salt. There's another door on the opposite wall. It's open just a crack.

"You know, Gina, you just sounded like Steve," Mary sounds sulky as I step toward the door to crane my head into the tiny hallway. The door on the end, leading to the bar area is propped open. Sid, the bouncer, who has forearms fat around as bowling pins, stands guard at the front door, which is opposite of the hallway. If he were to look straight ahead, I'd be busted.

"Listen Mare, the more you follow the rules your mom sets for you, the more she seems to make," I mutter over my shoulder. "Breaking a few here and there—"

"I do break the rules. I'm never home for supper—"

When a large man in a tweed blazer blocks Sid's view of the hallway, I slip out of the room, tugging Mary by her sleeve. Beaver Bedlam's cracker barrel beats and the barroom racket shatter my eardrums as we scuttle past the bar area.

"I'll be on a bender, honey, 'til the day you come back my waaay," the singer's twangy vocals ring over the THUMP-BOOM-THUMP of the rhythm section. Sweat and heat choke the air as we nudge our way through the tangle of bodies. My foot is nearly crushed by the man in the tweed blazer whose eyes are so fixed on his woman, he doesn't notice.

I pull my foot out from under him, cringing as I inch toward the dance floor, Mary at my heels. We snag the only table left, wobbly and half-hidden behind an amp. Its seats are duct-taped. I plop down, offer Mary a Winston, light one for myself, then slouch against the wall, putting on my best bored expression while two men wearing flannel shirts leer at us from a nearby table.

Mary remains on the edge of her seat, darting her eyes about. She cranes her neck at the raised stage, at the Beaver Bedlam Boys' singer who looks nine months pregnant. Mary wrinkles her nose at the moosehead, staring out at the room with its glass eyes from above the stage—maybe it's spying on us. Mary, shifting her attention to the leering men, wrinkles her nose and leans in toward me.

"Ew!" She shouts over the music, making a gagging gesture.

"Mary, you gotta act older!" I shout back.

"Whatta ya mean?"

"Act like you belong here."

"I am acting like I belong here." Mary looks annoyed.

John Hanlon, looking his John Hanlon best in a greasy New York Yankees baseball hat, worn backwards, lurches his way through the crowd and toward us. I roll my eyes.

Mary looks confused and worried.

I shake my head."Tell him you have permission

to be here if he asks—"

"Good evenin' ladies!" John stumbles into the table. Mary presses herself into the wall when he nearly falls into her lap. She shoots me a questioning look.

"Say it, don't spray it." I wipe John's spittle from my cheek.

Mary, still pressed against the wall, finds it in herself to laugh at my joke, but then she folds her arms across her chest when he stares at her cleavage.

"I'm John!" He offers her his hand.

His breath is so boozy, I'm scared to light a cigarette. It might cause an explosion. But I probably don't have to worry about him ratting me out. He's too drunk to know what's going on, or to be insulted as Mary pulls her sleeve over her hand before reaching out to shake his.

"Gina, baby, how's my pal?!" His beard tickles my cheek when he leans in to hug me. His breath smells warm and yeasty.

"Fine." I jerk away.

"Elaine here?"

I shrug.

"What're you gals doin' here?"

Mary's eyes widen.

"Watching the Suzi Bowman band." I kick her under the table.

"The Suzi who?" He presses closer. More spittle. His breath is horrendous.

"Suzi. Bowman. Band!" I yell over the music, getting impatient as I hold my breath in order to avoid another whiff of his.

"I ain't never heard 'o them."

"They're next."

"So they'll be on 'round nine-thirty. It's nine-fifteen now—oh, hey, kiddo, you ain't even 'posed to be here. Not without Elaine—"

"John, please don't tell anyone we're here, okay? Especially don't say nothing to Elaine. She'd shit a bird if she found out—"

"She'd shit a bird if she found out," John mocks, howling with laughter.

He thinks it's funny, but it's true. Elaine hardly ever cares about my comings and goings, but being in the Wrench, at night when she's not around, is off limits. It's not the law she worries about, it's more about the way she's seen some men act when they drink.

"You won't tell anyone, will you?"

John leans forward, his tenor voice tickling my eardrum. "I won't if you promise me a dance—"

"Come off it, John." I mash out my cigarette. Whether he's serious or jiving is beside the point. He's gross, and I wish'd he'd find some forty-year-old toothless tavern slut to get a hard on with, instead of two girls young enough to be his daughters.

"Dance one of these fast numbers with me." He jerks his pelvis in an attempt at some sort of Michael Jackson dance move. He's wiry like Michael but to me he looks like a scummy scarecrow that'd stumbled out of a corn field."How 'bout this one?"

"One dance and then leave me alone. I wanna hang out with my friend." I steal a glance around the room.

"Where're you going, Gina?" Mary sits with her knees drawn to her chest. Something she does whenever she feels insecure.

I lean into her ear. "I'm gonna go up with Bozo for one song and then I'll be sure to lose him."

When we reach the dance floor, I notice, for the first time, how much taller he is than me. His glass eye looks like the ones on my stuffed animals—the ones on Chuck's trout—shiny and dazed. The other eye is blood-shot and pointed at my boobs like a laser beam.

The song ends the moment we dance, so I shrug and slink away.

"Whoa, whoa, where you goin'?" John shouts over the cheers.

"My table."

"I ain't had that dance."

"You'll have to wait." I point at the crowd, now leaving the dance floor as the singer shouts, "Thank you and good night!"

John's glass eye looks frozen and dumb, but his real one blazes with anger. He storms off as the noise dies down.

"Who was that?" Mary asks as I sit.

"A regular." It's nice to talk without having to shout.

"He's creepy." She looks me in the eye.

"You think so?" I pretend to be surprised and we both laugh. "Are you having fun?"

She shrugs. "Not really, but it's okay."

"I got rid of him."

"It's okay, Gina. I'm doing this for you."

"Doing this for me? Tonight's supposed to be about us. I thought us sneaking out for old-time's sake would get you out of your rut."

"I'm not in a rut." She sounds annoyed. "I just don't sneak into bars unless I'm with Steve—by the way, we finally did it last night." Pride flashes in her eyes. "I picked him up at his workplace and he rented us a room at the Super 8, in Albany...."

"Wow." I chew my lip, thinking that I'm doomed to be a virgin until I'm forty.

"Hurt like hell, at first, but then after it was really awesome! And he licked me—down there."

I wrinkle my nose.

"Oh, Gina. That's the best part."

An image of Ellen, knocked up and couch surfing, with everything she owned spilling from the tops of Glad bags, pops into my mind. "You and Steve used a rubber, I hope."

"Uh...no, actually." Mary suddenly looks uncertain.

"That's crazy—"

"He pulled out in time."

"Congratulations." I grunt, lighting a Winston, wondering if I'd be losing my own cherry any time soon—not because I'm ready to—but because it's not cool to still be a virgin. I know, from having eavesdropped on the gossip girls at Chatswick that just about everyone's done it at least once.

Elaine tells me nothing about sex, and I feel dumb asking. She'll only talk about it after she's had a few, and that's only to brag about what she's done and with whom—stuff I'd rather not hear about—and her tone makes it seem like the pleasure's for the guys. She told me once that she needed to get buzzed before getting laid.

Suzi Bowman takes the stage. With her pixie hair and heavily made up eyes, she's as amazing to look at as I remembered. Her leather jacket and fifties, sock hop skirt makes her look like she's from another world, especially among all the baseball caps and flannel shirts. People on the dance floor are looking at her as if she's just pulled up in a spaceship instead of a car.

I give a hearty cheer as her band breaks into a bluesy, rockabilly tune. Couples try to dance, but they don't know quite what to do with their feet. The Two-step they'd used during the Beaver Bedlam Boys' set, doesn't fit the Suzi Bowman sound.

Mary joins me on the floor. We dance. She stops dancing suddenly, looks straight ahead, over my shoulder and sneers. The look on her face makes it seem like she just smelled a dead body or something. When I turn, John is there, trying to dance with us. Mary slinks to the other side of the floor. I follow, trying to blend in with the drunk, feathered-haired chicks, all dancing in a big circle.

Suzi uses heavy, downward strokes. The tempo picks up. I close my eyes and nod to the music, letting the sound wrap itself around me. Edgy bass lines boom in my chest, and my body becomes lighter and lighter, until I feel like I can fly—the instruments have their own individual colors. The bass is blue and the drums red...and I picture myself playing on that stage, bathed in red-violet lighting—

Something brushes my ass. I wheel around. John is there, flashing me a nasty grin.

"Don't you fucking touch me!"

"Have you forgotten the dance you promised?"

"Get away! I mean it, John!" I glance around. Everyone's too lost in the music to notice what's happening, except Mary who backs away—to our table, like it's her sanctuary—watching the scene like a scared rabbit.

"What're you gonna do 'bout it? Tell on me? You ain't even 'posed to be here." John lolls his tongue at me. It looks like a dead slug come to life between those rotten stumps for teeth. He slinks off.

"Come on, Gina. Let's just go," Mary says when I return to the table.

"No fucking way. I came to see this band!" Someone pokes my shoulder. When I wheel around, Sid is there, jerking his thumb at us to leave.

I zig zag my way toward the door, swishing past people, Mary clumsily following at my heels. John's sipping a Pabst and chatting with Sid when we reach the door. I slap the can out of his hand, catching a glimpse of the foam as it explodes on his T-shirt, on my way out.

"What the shit?!" He cries, his good eye stupefied.

"Elaine's gonna hear about this!" Sid's oven mitt-sized hands remain at his sides but his veins bulge like two blue, angry night crawlers under the skin of his temples. "Never come here again!" He slams the door behind us.

"Hope you're not mad at me," Mary whines, unlocking the driver's side door to the Corvette while I sit on the front bumper, smoking and staring at the trees. "Come on, Gina, get in." She pokes her head out the window. "Let's go for a drive, it's still early. Gina, let's catch a movie. Gina—"

Shut up, Mary.

I blow smoke into the night, my heart pounding so hard it drowns out the sound of footsteps crunching on the gravel.

"Gina!" I hear Mary shriek as a beefy hand snatches the back of my blouse. It rips as I break free from John's grasp and reach for the passenger door handle. I try to shut the door but he's already partway in. The door makes a dull banging sound as I get him in the hips.

"Ouch! Little whore!" He pulls back.

"Leave her alone!" I hear Mary scream when John comes for me again.

I hear a car horn, but it sounds far away. My hand feels far away and no longer attached to the rest of me. It slips from the handle as I try closing the door again.

John is now inside the car, causing it to reek of something awful—something rank—like beer and man-sweat. My head bounces off the steering wheel as John pins me down, his body heavy like a boulder. There's this squirming movement underneath my head as Mary tries to get out from under the weight of John and me.

His filthy nails puncture the skin on my chest, and I can feel the necklace Elaine gave me slither off my neck.

How dare him! I want to squeeze that glass eye out of his head and keep it for a souvenir. Better yet, squeeze the good one out of his head so he'll never be able gawk at young girls again. I knee him in the balls as he's going for my bra strap.

Mary continues to lay on the horn, while John, his face gone bone gray, slides off me, holding his crotch like a little boy ready to whiz himself. He looks ready to vomit.

I slam the door and lock it as John curls in a fetal position on the ground. I find the necklace between the seats, by the shifter. The chain's broken but the tiny stone is still intact.

Mary stops blowing the horn. "Someone help us, please," she cries to no one in particular, not noticing the blue lights that have surrounded us.

I'm barely aware of the cops, one lingering outside Mary's window, the other rapping on mine. All that goes through my mind, as I stare at the tiny stone, tucked in the crease of my palm, is how pissed I am about having broken the only family heirloom.

****

At the police station, Officer Goddard hammers me with a ton of questions, none of which I have answers for, because my memory of everything is one big blank.

"Gina wanted to see Suzy Bowman perform." Mary's cheeks are blotchy from crying. She looks at me. "I knew sneaking in would be a bad idea."

"Mr. Hanlon's been booked," says Goddard. "And a no-contact-order will be issued...Ms. Laramee?"

I stare at Goddard, standing in his office, on the other side of the counter, on the other side of the glass. He's a giant compared to the desk and everything else around him, including the eight-drawer file cabinet. I realize for the first time how big and fat his head is. Maybe I ought lop it off and shoot hoops with it.

"Are you alright?" He asks when I burst out laughing.

I half-nod, half-shake my head as the laughs turn to silent tears and I pull the blanket he'd given me around my shoulders, to hide my blouse, now looking like a torn surrender flag.

Officer Watts strolls in. He, too, practically swallows the tiny office, only his head seems much smaller than Goddard's. "Hi, Gina. Hi, Mary. Thought I recognized you two." He gives a half-smile, probably remembering us from last summer when he nearly booked us for trespassing on private property, and me for indecent exposure. Mary, her cousin, and I'd been playing Truth or Dare. Mary talked me into climbing Beckett's only fire tower, buck naked. "Your folks are on their way."

"I knew sneaking in would be a bad idea—"

"Can I smoke in here?"

Officer Goddard gives me a sour look.

Mary and I sit on the hard metal chairs, lined against the wall. I sigh, gazing down at the gleaming white floor that smells of ammonia. The scratches on my neck and shoulders sting like hell.

"I knew sneaking in would—"

"Shut up, Mary."

Mrs. Blum gusts through the glass double doors, her pajamas poking from the bottom of her parka, her brows furrowed, her cheeks pink from the cold. "Are you two okay?" She hugs Mary. "You stink like cigarettes."

I refuse to get up. Mrs. Blum bends down to hug me but I stiffen from her touch.

"Mary, you told me you were going to the movies." She suddenly looks pissed.

Mary starts bawling.

"My fault. My idea," I mumble.

Mrs. Blum says nothing. Her eyes are glued on Elaine, who trundles in, smelling of cocktails and sporting a belly dance costume, her jewelry jingling and shimmering under the fluorescent overheads. A plastic ruby screams from her belly button. Her false eyelashes are coming unglued. One dangles from her heavily rouged cheek. She told me earlier she was going to Sharon's costume party.

There's anger, but there's fear in her eyes, too, as she stands in front of me, her shoulders stooped, her arms limp at her sides as she stares down at me, not saying anything. "You little shit," she says, finally, almost whispering, her voice quivering. "I've told you before: stay away from the men. You get what you deserve when you put yourself in that situation."

Mary's eyes bug. Her jaw drops.

"Elaine, that's not fair," Mrs. Blum gasps.

I glance through the partitioned window, hoping Goddard will clue Elaine in on what happened, but he's gone and Mr. Watts is on the phone with his back to us.

"Get your ass out to the car." Elaine yanks me by my elbow. The necklace slips from my hand. Dumbfounded and shocked, I stoop over to pick it up, not once looking at Mary and her mother as we leave.

****

It's still dark when I pack quickly and quietly by placing my guitar in a Glad trash bag, before glancing one last time at my stuffed animals, the banner I got on a seventh-grade field trip to the Boston Aquarium, and my pom-pom fringed curtains. A pang hits me when I see the Joy Division album, still on my turn table. I hate to leave my records behind and wonder, as I glance at my rumpled bed, where the heck I'll be sleeping tonight. The knob feels cool under my palm as I close my door and am swallowed by the dark.

I creep along the hall, careful not to bump into Elaine's stupid rockstar photos. Chuck's snores leak through the thin walls. They sound like the neighbor's lawn mower and are punctuated by his baritone farts.

In the glow of the stove light, I find a set of Ernie Ball guitar strings on the counter. Elaine knew I needed new ones—it's probably another one of her 'I'm sorry for last night' presents—for the fight we'd had the night before, the one that started over cold pizza. I wonder what kind of present I'll get after having been blamed for nearly getting raped by John, the cheesy mood ring he gave her for her birthday?

It looks like Elaine shopped for food. I snag a box of Nature Valley granola bars and several cans of Hawaiian Punch. The fridge smells fishier than ever. The trout heads are still there, on a plate, on top of the crisper drawer. Their eyes have sunken into their heads, now dull and flaky, their lips frozen in mute horror. I snag the entire pound of bologna and the half pound of American cheese from the top shelf, and the loaf of Big Daisy bread from the top of the fridge, along with Elaine's carton of mentholated Newports and fifty dollars from her purse.

A Polaroid of Elaine and me hangs on the fridge. We were at Lake George the day Billy'd taken the photo. Elaine, her flaming hair piled in a bun, wore mirrored shades and a terri-cloth striped bikini, while I sported a green one-piece and a goofy grin as I squinted for the camera. Elaine is smiling down at me, a genuine smile, her arm draped across my shoulders. I'd never felt closer to her before or since that day.

The photo almost makes me lose my nerve, even though I've seen it a million times—until I see the cloud of fruit flies floating aimlessly above Chuck's empty Schlitz cans, piled next to the snake cage. Lenny and Squiggy are dead to the world as they lie coiled like garden hoses under the heat lamp. I grab my things and slip out.

On the stoop, wobbly from dry rot and covered in frost, I glance one last time at the sagging, moss-covered tool shed and the lone bird feeder—with no bird feed—dangling from the roof, and the lawn so overgrown, it could win the blue ribbon at any redneck contest.

Now what?

The dark sky fades to a silver-yellow in the East as I shield myself from the wind by walking backwards, slowly, away from my trailer and toward the end of Dwight Street, Elaine's Cutlass growing smaller and smaller, until it becomes a brown dot in the distance. My hands shake as I light a Newport before pausing on the iron bridge— the kind that makes a humming sound when cars drive over it, and crosses the Piska River in order to join the trailer park to the mainland.

The gray water, which stinks of rotten eggs, snakes its way along the sludgy banks. A steamy little cloud tumbles from my lips when I laugh, but the laugh doesn't sound like mine. It sounds like it's coming from someone else. My heart pounds as I toss my butt over the rail, then head for the main drag, waving my thumb to the oncoming cars.

Part Two

"Port Authority! Port Authority!" The driver barks as the Peter Pan rolls into a cool, concrete building, then hisses to a stop. He kills the engine and steps off. I sit frozen in my seat as the bus clears fast.

Grabbing my stuff, finally, I mutter, "Thank you," to the driver, but he doesn't hear me. He's shouting directions to the people continuing on to Philadelphia. Going to Philadelphia would be nice, not because I want to go to Philadelphia, but because I'm not ready to leave my womb on wheels.

Tasting exhaust fumes on my tongue, I let my eyes adjust to the darkness of the station. Cold air slaps my neck as I numbly watch the other passengers bumble about, trying to get at their suitcases, heaped on the oil-stained concrete. Light splashes in from a row of doors leading inside the station—I've heard creepy stories about Port Authority. Billy told me once that the prostitutes and homeless people weren't the worst part about the station, when I'd asked him to take me on a trip to New York. He told me it was the strange things he'd seen. Once, he saw a severed finger in the urinal of the men's room.

Instead of going inside, I let the dim lighting of this clammy cave guide me toward the sunlight, seeping in from where the bus pulled in. The noon sun burns my eyes. A fire truck screams past, and I almost get clipped by a taxi when I step off the curb. The driver, wearing a funny towel thing on his head, blasts his horn at me.

Safely on the other side, I lean against a building to smoke a cigarette, watching all the weird people go by. A man, wearing one of those hats Jewish men wear, bumps me with his briefcase while waving down a cab. Everyone's in a hurry and I'm in the way. In order not to feel in the way, I follow the human current for a couple blocks and end up in a big square full of electric ads.

On an island, between the lanes of traffic, looms the biggest Coca Cola sign I've ever seen. White, cursive lettering shimmers on a background of neon red, telling me to Enjoy Coke! I look for a place to sit but am distracted by more billboards: Jordache Jeans, Fuji Film, Panasonic, TDK Audio & Video Cassettes. It's dizzying. There's a movie house featuring "The Evil Dead." Mary and I were supposed to go see that on Halloween.

I wander down a less crowded street, stopping to light a cigarette in front of a shop entrance framed in stuttering red lights:

XXX RATED
GIRLS, GIRLS, GIRLS
THIS WEEK'S FEATURE:
GLORIA GASH
THIS HOT AND HORNY
HONEY IS HOT TO TROT!!!

Totally naked, except for her silver stilettos, Gloria has bleached hair and a fake tan—the kind that comes in a tube and turns your skin orange—and three gold stars: one over her crotch, the other two over her nipples. Her lips, puckered in an O, suggest a BJ.

A woman, sporting thigh-high boots and spandex shorts that are so short her cheeks are spilling out the bottoms, strolls by with a man in a business suit on her arm. They enter the hotel next door.

"Psst, hey!!!" A boy, probably not older than ten, with large intense eyes mutters, "Reefer, reefer, reefer. Good Mexican...getcha real high...got blow too if reefer ain'tcher thing."

Not sure I know what blow is, I only stare at the boy, nearly banging into an Asian couple as I walk away. But the boy follows me. "Psst! You gotta dollar? You gotta smoke?"

I give him a Newport, not bothering to light it for him, but then feel bad about giving him a cigarette 'cause he's a little kid. But I quickly forget about him and the hooker and the stripper with the fake tan when I catch a whiff of fried food—a nice break from the smell of urine and garbage. A yellow, neon sign ahead says:

GRAY'S PAPAYA
SPECIAL
TWO FRANKS, ONE DRINK
$2.50

The tiny diner has no seating, just a shallow counter you stand at, but the sound of the sizzling grill and Men at Work's "Down Under," drifting from the boom box, behind the register, is comforting, and a break from the noise of traffic. While eating, I gaze out the window, at the steam rising from a sewer drain and the pigeons that bobble along the lip of the curb, pausing to peck at soda cups, cigarette butts and other trash. New York's different from the way I'd pictured it, especially after having seen every episode of *Fame*. It's actually grimier, less flashy....

I think of my mother. Is she alive? What's she like as a person? Where's she living, exactly—New York's huge. I saw just how huge when the bus snaked its way through the Bronx. The Peter Pan bus felt like an ant among all those brick high rises. Mostly, I wonder why it is she never came back for me, if she ever thinks about me. I finger the velvet box like a worry stone. The broken necklace is inside of it. The box sits deep in the pocket of my windbreaker.

I swallow hard, pushing the thought of Ellen away by keeping my eyes peeled for limousines, wondering if I'll see somebody famous—maybe later I'll try to look for Juilliard—after I find somewhere to sleep. I don't know what I was thinking, coming down here like this. Maybe being gone a couple of days'll be enough to scare the crap out of Elaine and then—

"You look pretty today," a man in black jeans and a crisp white shirt talks to me. He's standing on my left, watching me lick the sweet relish, oozing from the ends of the bun. "You alright, sugar? You look kinda lost."

"I'm not lost." I straighten. He's eying my guitar. I push it closer to me with my foot.

"Am I making you uncomfortable?"

"No." The hotdog tasted better before he got

here.

"You look like you need a place to stay."

"Know of any cheap rooms that aren't gross?" I look at the man for the first time.

"This is New York, baby, not some Podunk town where you came from."

"What makes you think—?"

"Sugar, sweet things like you pass through here everyday." He flashes a smile. His teeth are weird. They're too white and too even. "You aren't gonna find a bed in your price range, I can guarantee you that...but, a beautiful girl like you does have resources." He clicks his tongue, his eyes roaming my body, stopping only when they notice the frayed ends of my shirt sleeves. "Aren't you tired of those old clothes?"

"What…resources?" I look at him sideways. There's something cold and dirty about his eyes and it makes me queasy, even though the dogs'd been delicious. I glance at the last bite, drowning in a pool of catsup on my paper plate.

"When you get good and tired of living on the streets, gimme a call." He flashes another smile, slipping me a business card, black with gold raised letters.

Mitch Z.
FILM PRODUCER

When I look up, he's already on the street. Not once does he look back at me.

****

It sure was dumb of me, coming down here with no plan, thinking I'm gonna meet famous people and find Ellen—a woman with blue-green eyes like mine who could give two sucks about me. Daylight's fading, and I don't know where I am because I'm too scared to ask anybody how to get to the Bowery—a place where people can rent rooms for five bucks. I read that once somewhere.

Even with a limp in my step, caused by a blister that burns at my right heel from having walked all afternoon, I walk faster—all the while dodging the mounds of garbage piled on the sidewalks, where rats rove soundlessly in the shadows of the boarded up brownstones—beetle in and out of the street lamp's dim lighting. The entire front wall of one building has collapsed, leaving the individual apartments in full view, with just a flimsy wall dividing each. It reminds me of a row of tonsils in a giant, yawning mouth. I hurry across the street, toward a park.

Inside the park, among a stand of trees, I find a bench, not far from three tents made of plywood and plastic tarp. Five people stand around a trash can fire that stinks of garbage and burning rubber. All I can make out of them is the craggy outline of their bodies, glowing orange by the light of the flames. Maybe they won't care if I sleep here.

But just as I'm about to lay on the bench, I notice that one of them wears a spiked dog collar and a leather ski mask with a zipper over the mouth. The collar is hitched to a leash and held by one very tall woman wearing a sequined gown and fur coat. Her lipstick contrasts with her heavy face, mottled with five o'clock shadow. It's rude to stare but I can't help it.

"That bitch is bad as fuck! That's my whole point!" The woman booms in a baritone voice, tipping a bottle to her lips.

I hurry out of the park and onto the street, sidestepping shattered glass on the sidewalk, my pace quick, my chest thrust forward, my head held high, even as my heart bangs wildly. My mouth feels dry and cottony and I hear drumbeats, followed by the shriek of a synthesizer and the whine of an electric guitar, and assume it's someone, somewhere, blaring a radio from a glassless window, in one of these dumpy buildings. The sounds grow louder as I continue for about a block or two, before realizing that the music is actually live and coming from a building on the other side of an abandoned lot. Crossing the lot choked with weeds is scary, but so is going back the way I came. So is continuing on, where all city light cuts out completely and I'm at the mercy of the moonlight, which curves around the buildings, splashing the sidewalk in patches. But what about the hiccups of blackness in between the patches of light? It is inside these hiccups, where no light reaches, that I expect, at any moment, to be grabbed and dragged into one of the buildings—earlier, I heard someone whistle 'Yo, baby,' at me from a doorway.

The music grows louder. I decide to cross the lot. Traces of human lives are dumped and forgotten among the tall grass: a steam radiator next to a broken dresser with its bottom drawer popping out like a tongue, a rusty shower stall leaning drunkenly against an upright piano, Goldenrod sprouting where the piano's keys used to be. A few yards in front of me, I spot two people, slumped in the backseat of a junked Buick, one bobbing his head in an and down motion. I'm not sure what they're up to, exactly, but a sick feeling settles in my stomach as I hurry toward the building.

The outside is plastered with graffiti. I do a loop around the building, getting a good look in the dim light. There are animals and cartoons covering the entire north wall. The west wall displays an alligator with a face like Ronald Reagan. The Reagan-like alligator is shown to be gobbling up homeless people as he crawls out of a manhole. Above, spray-painted in red drips reads:

POVERTY IS AN URBAN MYTH.

I stuff my guitar and Jansport bag in the tall weeds, then walk toward a cement stairwell that smells like puke. It leads to the basement, to a black steel door with the word SOMEWHERE painted in big, white letters. There are no windows at this level, and the windows on the first, second, third and fourth floors are bricked over.

Three guys come through the metal door, bringing with them a wall of earsplitting music, cigarette smoke and heat. They thud up the stairs in black combat boots.

I back away, but they don't seem to see me. They look around, as if looking for something or someone. One has slicked black hair and eyes lined heavily with makeup. His skin is so chalky he looks like death riding in on a motorcycle with that black leather jacket of his and leather boots. His movements, as he lights a thin brown cigarette, are slow and easy in a way that make him seem catlike. An earthy, peppery smell floats on the air as he lets the smoke roll out his nostrils.

He catches me staring. My pulse flutters and I feel myself blush while running a hand through my hair, embarrassed by how dirty it is. He gives me a cold look.

"Is this a tavern?" I blurt, but he doesn't seem to hear me as he passes the cigarette to his friend, who sports a pea coat and has the reddest hair I've ever seen. The redhead looks at me like I have spiders crawling out of my ears when I ask, "Where am I?"

The third friend, with frizzy hair and a denim jacket says, "You're Somewhere, man," and laughs. "Just kidding, this is an art gallery. Bands play here sometimes... most people don't know about it—"

"We like to keep it that way," the redhead snorts, spitting a lunger on the ground. He nods to the black-haired friend. The two head down the steps.

"I heard music and just thought...uh...sorry I asked," my voice cracks.

"Wait!" Mr. Frizz calls out to me as I turn away. "You can come in, man." He jerks a thumb at the staircase. "No big deal. Don't pay any attention to my friends, they're assholes...name's Danny." Mr. Frizz holds out his hand.

I hesitate.

"Danny." He looks at me expectantly, so I shake it. It's sweaty.

"Gina."

"Just go down those steps—"

"I know."

"Right. If anybody asks—no one will—but if they do, tell 'em you're a friend of the Weird Sisters...they're one of the bands playing tonight. They sort of run the place."

"Oh." A half-smile wavers on my lips as I hold back tears. The last person to talk to me was a hooker in the subway, and that was only to bum a light from me. I hadn't realized how lonely I was.

****

The entire basement, including its low ceilings and pipes, are painted black. The hard, driving beats and scraping guitars are deafening. The air is warm, heavy and smells like sweat. The cement floors are sticky, and the only light comes from a set of black lights, illuminating three, enormous, black and white canvases suspended above two, tattered couches.

The first canvas is a collage made up of mug-shots and fingerprints, the second looks like a series of barcodes, and the third looks like an inkblot test. A young woman with a buzz hair cut, lies on one of the couches, under the inkblot canvas, her head in the black-haired friend's lap and her feet on the redhead's.

"What's wrong!?" Danny shouts in my ear. I spin around, dumping someone's drink, which'd been sitting on the edge of a table, onto my loafer.

Crap.

"No worries Gina, that person left," Danny continues to yell over the music, a dopey grin peering out from under his frizzy bangs.

"You remember my name." I'm surprised he's talking to me again.

"Well, why wouldn't I?"

"Thanks for coming out!" An Asian-looking girl, sporting a Mohawk, taps Danny's shoulder. The entire bust section of her dress has been cut out, then replaced and stitched together with clear plastic. I can see her nipples. I hadn't meant to show such surprise and instantly feel dumb, not that it matters, since she's already halfway toward the exit, her bass slung over one shoulder, banging against her hip as she climbs the stairs.

"That girl...her uh...thingies were, uh...."

"Showing? That's the latest fashion." Danny grins. "Where you from? Upstate?" He points at my gray sweat shirt with the words SYRACUSE UNIVERSITY stitched across the chest. "You don't look like you're from around here."

"Can anybody be from around here?" I make a screwy face. The city, especially this part, seems too dirty and crazy and wild for anybody to be from here—although it is kind of beautiful, in a strange sort of way...maybe because it is dirty and crazy and wild.

"Good point. This is the transplant capital, but some people are even less from around here than others...does that make sense?"

I furrow my brows.

"If you stick around long enough, you too'll start to look like you're from around here compared to those just passing through."

"But even if I were to stick around long enough, it still wouldn't mean that I was from around here."

Danny smiles. His teeth glow purple in the lighting. "That sort of rhetoric comes from people who are just passing through."

The black-haired friend pulls the buzz-haired girl into an upright position while the redhead presses a cup to her lips. The girl pushes the cup away and pukes. The puddle, pooling at her feet in front of the couch, glows pink in the black lighting.

"Stan and Jeff are cleaning it up this time." Danny wrinkles his nose, his voice dropping to normal as the music cuts out. "Cripes, if Joni keeps that shit up, the Weird Sisters aren't gonna want her hanging around here no more...every time she snorts dope, that happens...oh, hey, I gotta go, Gina. My band's up next."

I try to follow Danny up the stairs, but am assaulted by the strobe lights and The Talking Heads, blaring at full volume. The entire first floor looks as if Gallagher had come through and worked the place over with his mallet. Only instead of melon running down the brick walls, it's dried paint spatters and large, looping graffiti scrawl. I'm thirsty for a pop but can't see where there's a bar, not that it matters since I can't get any further than the top of the stairs.

Danny's back melts into the crowd and I find myself alone and out of place in my loafers and Syracuse sweat-shirt among the suit jackets and skinny ties, gelled hair and tribal make up. I inch my way toward the back, to-ward the pool table, where there's less strobe lighting, my eyes burning from the cigarette smoke.

I lean against a steel post, putting on my best bored expression while pretending to be interested in the game of pool, even though neither of the players are any good. The woman with white face paint and black eye-shadow scratches every other shot. Her opponent, a two-hundred pound-black dude wearing leather chaps and a gold ring in his nose, seems not to remember whether he is play-ing stripes or solids.

"Gotta smoke I can bum?" Danny springs from out of nowhere, wearing that dopey grin. "Ah...menthols are the best," he says when I light a Newport for him. He inhales deeply, his grin broadening as he scrawls something on a matchbook cover. I shoot him a hopeful look when he hands me the it.

"The address to the Stigmatas' rehearsal space," he says when I try to read his handwriting.

"Stigmatas...rehearsal space?" My heart sinks. It's not a place to crash.

"Our band." Danny points to his redheaded friend, who stands on an amp, flipping people off. Projected onto a screen behind him is a grainy, homemade-looking film, showcasing close ups of goldfish swimming in lazy circles. "We're rehearsing tomorrow. You should stop by." Danny slips away, his frizzy hair bouncing to the tune of his clumsy gait as a squeal of feedback cuts in.

I lean against the post, my hands clapped over my ears, grinding my teeth as the dark-haired friend churns out another squeal of feedback by tipping his bass to the amplifier. The music they play, if you can call it that, is like listening to a car crash...I mean we're talking a really shitty version of the Cramps. Now, picture a really shitty version of the Cramps but fronted by Ornette Coleman under the influence of model airplane glue and you basically have the Stigmatas.

Danny thrashes his tom tom and snare with a pair of wire whisks, while his black-haired friend repeats the same two chords on his out-of-tune bass. The red head's saxophone solos sound like the mating cries of an Orca. In between solos, he bounces on the balls of his feet, while sing-shouting, "Can't get down off the floor. Can't get up down the ceiling...." in a braying donkey voice, goldfish projected onto his torn, white T-shirt.

Goldfish tails flap on Danny's pale forehead. They zip along the dark-haired friend's midriff. He seems oblivious to the fish, as well as the audience, now forming a silhouette on the film projection as they dance. Or try to. Their feet don't sync with the music, never mind the rest of their bodies. Instead, they move in one, throbbing pulse, like one giant, vibrating jellyfish.

I can't help but smile. It's not like I'm laughing at them. I'm not, it's just...I don't know what to make of it all...I guess I could dance too if I wanted to, without worrying whether I look good, and at least I no longer have to worry about my ugly, hick clothes or about being here alone, or that I have an ugly haircut, because no one here cares. For the first time since I've arrived, I'm not scared....

Soon, I find myself moving to the music, to the noise, or whatever it is.

****

When the music stops, I look for Danny, but the place is even more jammed. I get elbowed in the face twice as I make my way toward the stairs. A deep exhaustion catches up with me when I reach the basement and don't see Lenny there either.

The boys are halfway across the abandoned lot when I step outside. My breath makes steamy jets in the chilled air as I shout to Danny, who keeps walking, his back to me, obviously not hearing me. Or maybe he can hear me...? The three boys vanish into the shadows.

It's 4:00 a.m. and the lot is deathly quiet, now that the music has stopped, even though there are more people outside now than there were when I came in.

****

A nudge to the ribs stirs me from my sleep. I blink, expecting to see my pompom curtains, stuffed animals and Elaine's puffy face looming over mine, barking, 'I'm not driving you to school if you miss the bus!' Instead, the memories of last night: the club, the weird music and now this grimy shopfront, snaps me awake. A clerk in a black jumpsuit and patent leather pumps, like the ones in the window of the shop I'm plunked in front of, jingles her keys impatiently as I peel my cold and achey self off the cement. Right now, I'd be in gym class getting socked in the stomach with a dodgeball, alongside the Bearded Lady—no. Today's Sunday, not Monday. Right now, I'd be knocking on Mary's door to see if she was around. Instead, I'm standing over a subway grate, warming myself with the dank, smelly air that wafts from the station below. Tears threaten as I feed dimes to the pay phone and dial home, noticing how quickly the sky has clouded over. I chicken out after the first ring and hang up. Drawing a deep breath, I dial the Blum's.

"Holy crap, Gina. Where are you? I'm hearing lots of sirens!" I barely hear Mary's voice over the firetruck and the subway, now roaring into the station under my feet.

"Watch your mouth, Mary," I overhear Mrs. Blum scold. I didn't realize she was on the other line. Part of me feels comforted by this, part of me feels annoyed.

"What, Ma? Least I didn't say shit. Geez—"

"Now you just said shit when I told you not to say crap...and don't take the Lord's name in vain."

"I didn't take the Lord's name in vain. I said

geez."

"Well, you may as well have been taking the Lord's name in vain when you said geez—"

"Who cares, Ma—"

"Mary, just hang up. I'll handle this—"

"But, Ma—"

"Don't *Ma* me...Gina?"

"Gina?!" Mary yells in the background, "Come home."

"Mary!" Mrs. Blum bawls.

"Jeezum Crow!"

I hold the receiver away from my ear while Mrs. Blum bawls Mary out in that drilling voice of hers. When I hear CLUNK CLUNK I worry that we've been disconnected.

"Gina, what've you done?" Mrs. Blum says a moment later, sounding out of breath.

"I—"

"You're not in Beckett."

"Uh—"

"Where are you?"

"Uh—"

"Tell me where you are. I'll come get you—"

"Mrs. Blum, I don't really...." The tears start when I think about how much I miss Mary and her mother but...I think about last night, about the art on the side of that building, and the music and the fashion—and the girl in that crazy get up, who shamelessly flashed her boobs—and Danny and feel torn.

"Either tell me where it is you've wandered to or I'll have the police look for you—"

I hang up.

****

The Stigmatas' rehearsal space is large and open and musty smelling. It looks like it could've been an industrial space at one time. A cold clamminess penetrates its brick walls. Naked bulbs dangle from high ceilings, where air ducts and heavy beams, clotted with cobwebs, shoot across. The floor-to-ceiling windows—some of the panes broken and sealed over with plastic—offer a distant view of the World Trade towers.

The rain picks up again and I can hear it pattering on the windows. At the opposite end of the room, the girl with the buzzed hair, from last night, sits at an easel under a glaring light. Not once does she look up.

"Gina, you made it." Danny smiles from behind his drum kit. He's fumbling with a cymbal that refuses to stay on its stand. The redhead, crouched in the corner, has his back to me and is fiddling with an extension chord.

"Hi," says a skinny girl, with small, shapeless lips, practically staring a hole through me. A gray pig on a leash sleeps at her Winnie-the-Pooh-slippered feet. "You look miserable. Take off your rain gear and sit." She makes room for me on the saggy love seat. I look hesitantly down at the pig, grunting in its sleep on the cement floor.

"Don't be afraid, Precious loves people... name's Desiree." The girl cracks her gum loudly, offering her hand. I shake it, thinking that this is the first time I ever shook hands with someone with a pet pig—come to think of it, Desiree's hands smell of pig, although they probably smell better than mine, which are grimy from the streets, despite the pink, chemical soap I'd washed them with while sponge bathing in a McDonald's restroom.

"Where'd you get the pig?" It's all I can think to say to Desiree—to anybody—since Danny seems more interested in adjusting his cymbal than having a conversation, which makes me wonder if he'd given me the address to be nice, all the while hoping I wouldn't actually drop by.

"I rescued her from a farm in Illinois," Desiree grows louder as Danny drowns us out with the crashing of his snare. "Where her mama was taken away and cruelly slaughtered by the members of the Carnivore Institute. That's what I call those bastards who slaughter animals for meat. Precious was a baby when I got her. Raised her myself. Fed her from a bottle...."

Desiree prattles on for the next half-hour on the politics of environmentalism, and about how she's taken a feminist stance by refusing to shave, her voice nearly drowned out by the elephant squeals of Jeff's sax. He's blowing the instrument inches away from her head while Precious remains dead to the world and Buzz Girl continues to paint. I squirm in the love seat, my soggy feet giving me the chills as a slight headache comes on.

It's a relief when the racket cuts out—having stopped the moment the dark-haired friend arrives with two waxed bags, soggy from the rain. The soles of his sneakers, which are drenched, make a squeaking sound as he crosses the room. His shaggy black bangs and the way his damp hair clings to the nape of his slender neck in perfect ringlets, makes my heart skip, and I can't resist staring at his watery, chalk-blue eyes, smudged with mascara. They seem to reflect the rain and the grayness of the world beyond the window.

"Hope you guys enjoy your dead animals," Desiree snorts.

The boys, now seated at the coffee table, unravel their heroes from the waxed paper.

"Americans eat more meat than any other country...."

No comment. Only the sound of rain and chewing.

"Animal poop is polluting our atmosphere...."
No comment.

"More and more trees gets wiped out each year, just to raise beef...."

Silence. Jeff farts.

"Just so you can eat—"

"Hey, Desiree, I reserved a little snack for Precious." The dark-haired friend wags a piece of bacon at Precious, now snoring. His voice sounds surprisingly deep, considering he's so skinny.

"Excuse me." She shoots out of the love seat, looking ready to cry as she pulls Precious up by the collar. The big gray sow, its torpedo-shaped body, which lay like a stone on the floor a moment ago, slowly rises on its squat legs, sneezes once and waddles after Desiree. The two lumber down the stairs, leaving a scent of patchouli and B.O. in their wake.

"Sorry, man," The dark-haired friend says to the red-head. "She never shuts up."

"I know."

"Why do you let her hang around?"

"She lives downstairs. It's not like I can get rid of her—"

"Dude, she doesn't wear deodorant. She doesn't shave her legs." The dark-haired friend wrinkles his nose.

The redhead shrugs. "She puts out."

"Yeah, but dude, her pits are so hairy you could hang a peace sign off 'em. If a chick's that hairy under the arms, I don't even wanna know what she's got down there—"

"Uh...I'm trying to eat, here." Danny shoots the dark-haired friend a look of disgust between bites of meatball. "Want some of my sandwich, Gina?"

"No thanks, Danny. Don't eat dead animals." I manage a grin.

"Ha!" He laughs. The other two look at me for the first time.

"Name's Gina." I give them a half wave but then shift uneasily in the love seat when they say nothing back.

"You boys wanna get stoned? I was waiting for Desiree to leave." Buzz Girl sets her paint brush down. Still wearing her smock, she comes over with a glass of water and a joint in her lips. The ring in her nose catches my eye.

"I like the artwork," I say to no one in particular, sitting on my hands to avoid fidgeting as I crane my neck at the collage hanging on the wall above the love seat, made up of body parts and faces of Cheryl Tiegs, Morgan Fairchild and Farrah Fawcett.

"I made that," says Buzz Girl.

The red-head takes the joint from Buzz Girl, drags deep and passes it to Danny. "Are you cool?" He says to me, smoke forming a lazy halo around his head.

"I...I don't know...yeah...I mean, I guess I'm cool...."

Buzz Girl eyes me, as if waiting for a better answer—Like what? No, I'm a narc? I cast my eyes to the floor, feeling like a toad, and about as wanted as Precious and Pig Girl.

The redhead chokes from trying not to laugh as he releases the smoke. "Dude," he says to his dark-haired friend. "She doesn't know what I'm talking about—"

"How can I know what the fuck you're talking about when I don't even know your fucking names?" The skin on my neck tightens.

Buzz Girl laughs a high tinkling laugh. The redhead looks vaguely surprised. The black-haired friend—slouching against the amp with a deadpan expression—says nothing. The redhead snickers and coughs again. I hate him. I hate all of them, even Danny for not having bothered to introduce us...for leaving last night without saying goodnight to me. He just sits there like a dimwit. Why'd he invite me?

The redhead nods to Danny, "Yup, she's cool."

Danny nods, taking a greedy pull from the joint, practically swallowing it with his blubbery lips before passing it to me. Not sure what do with it, I let it dangle loosely between my index and middle finger, slimy from Danny's spit.

"Babe," says the redhead. "You gonna sit there looking at it?"

"Name's Gina...so nice to finally meet you...." Asshole.

"Take it easy, man. Have a puff. It'll relax you. You look stiffer than a corpse in a body bag." The redhead says, standing on his tiptoes as he stretches his back, cracking his knuckles.

I drag on the joint like I would a cigarette, then hand it to the dark-haired friend. My chest hitches as I sputter and cough, smoke tumbling from my lips as a twinge of pain shoots up my ribs.

"I'm Joni." Buzz Girl hands me her glass of water, a hint of laughter in her eyes, knowing I'd never gotten high before. I don't care, I just want the coughing to stop. It does, and a warm dreamy feeling takes over. The rehearsal space becomes softer, fuzzier somehow, and I quickly forget about my wet feet.

"I'm Stan. Stan Jordan," says the dark-haired friend, his rainy, chalk-blue eyes, slightly amused as they look into mine for the first time. My body flushes as he points to the redhead, "This is Bozo the Clown."

"Kiss my ass, Jordan."

"You'd make a great Bozo with that red hair."

"Fine, just don't call me Little Debbie," the redhead snorts. His eyes, now red like his hair, have become two slits.

"Bozo's real name is Jeff, AKA Little Debbie—"

"Suck it, Jordan."

"Should we rehearse another song before calling it quits?" asks Danny. For a minute I thought he'd become mute.

"Sure...let's practice "No Eye Contact""? Stan stares into the air ducts as if angels are lurking among them.

"I don't wanna do that one." Jeff lights a cigarette. He begins pacing.

""Slim Jim?"" Danny offers, taking another toke off the joint, now a puny stub. ""Acid Casualties?""

""Magic Bullets."" Jeff stops pacing.

"We've played that one to death." Stan drags his eyes off the ceiling.

""Blender Dog,"" Joni offers, plopping down next to me.

At Joni's suggestion, the band breaks into a sludgy, distorted number. Danny throws down his drumsticks when feedback squeals from the amp. "Can we start that again?"

"Just play the song straight through, Danny," says Jeff.

"You're not following me at all, Stan," says Danny.

"You're tempo's too fast," says Stan.

"I wrote the song with the intention of it being slow, and slow is how I want it," says Jeff. "You wanna write songs, Danny, be my guest. We need more material anyway. I'm sick of doing all the work."

The Stigmatas break into a song, or, rather a series of feedback and noise, much like last night, only instead of playing the sax, Jeff plays a continuous crunchy guitar riff on a duct-taped Stratocaster, excess string coiling out of the headstock. Stan joins Jeff on the bass, playing the same two chords he played last night. He peters out in the middle of the song, asking, "Wait...what're we doing?"

Danny starts the song from the top again. Jeff sings something like, "Death to Little Debbie," in a voice that sounds like a seal going into labor. The music cuts out again when a freckled kid around my age, wearing an arm cast, shows up.

No one pays any attention to me when I pick up Jeff's Stratocaster. They're chatting with the freckled boy, but when I begin playing one of my originals, with no title and no lyrics, heads turn. Joni pokes Jeff, who stares at me in disbelief and then amusement as I begin using heavy down-strokes—playing faster than the guys had on any of their songs—losing myself in the pure enjoyment of Jeff's electric as I make a steely, warbling sound by dragging my lighter across the frets. The look of amusement fades from Jeff's face as he listens with an ear cocked, even as one of the strings breaks and I keep playing.

When I finish, the room is silent for a second until Danny shouts, "Whew! Smokin'!" His claps echo from the high ceiling. Joni fixes her gaze on me while Stan stares at his sneakers. Jeff's mouth hangs open.

"Sorry about your string," I tell Jeff, placing his guitar on its stand, my heart thumping from the adrenaline.

"Don't sweat it. All the others have gone out on me this week," Jeff says, resuming a bored front.

"I got an idea for the Stigmatas," the freckled boy says to Stan, while pointing at Jeff, "Fire Little Debbie and let your lady friend take over guitar—"

"Listen, here, you little fudge packer. D'you bring the money like I asked?"

"I'll lend it to you on one condition—"

"I hate conditions."

"Forget it, then." The boy turns away.

"Come off it, you little pecker head." Jeff snatches the boy by the hood of his sweatshirt.

"Here!" He stumbles backward, thrusting a twenty in Jeff's hand.

"Whoa...what're you, loaded?" Jeff's eyes bug. He releases the kid's hood. "So you're the little twerp with all the money. Those rich perverts pay you fat, do they?" He biffs the kid on the head playfully.

"Ouch, quit it. The condition is you gotta score me a gram too—"

"No fucking way." Jeff shakes his head. "Knowing your stupid ass, you'll get hooked. I don't want that shit on my head—"

"If you score for me, you won't have to pay me back."

Jeff looks thoughtful.

"And I won't get hooked, I swear—Dylan and I are throwing a party at his place. His mom and dad are away this week—"

"Dylan's parents trust that hoodlum by himself?" Jeff whistles under his breath.

"I promised to bring the stuff. It'll increase my

chances of getting laid—"

"If you're on that shit you may as well forget about using that dinger between your legs."

"I got it figured out...Tyler's gonna be there...been trying to get in his pants for weeks—"

"I'll do it this one time, but never again." Jeff pokes a finger in the kid's chest.

"You're awesome, Jeff." On his way out the door, the kid pauses, looks at me and says, "You're an awesome guitar player, whoever you are."

I smile.

Danny shoots Jeff a nasty look. "He's only thirteen, Jeff—"

"He'll just end up scoring from somebody else, Lenny." Jeff shrugs.

The room becomes silent, except for the rain hitting the window.

"Travis is a trip," Joni says suddenly.

"He's a little pecker head, but I love him," says Jeff. "He's had a hard time. His asshole folks kicked 'im out 'cause he's gay. Then a trick broke his arm...that's why he's got that cast." Jeff slips two twenty-dollar bills into his faded, leather wallet. "I'm calling it a day." He packs up his saxophone. Stan grabs his bass.

"We'll see you in a bit," Jeff tells Joni as she returns to her easel.

I watch the rain come down harder while Danny gathers the trash off the coffee table, shooting glances at me. "Gina, do you need a ride somewhere?"

Jeff's 1977, Dodge van is painted Day-Glo orange and covered with inverted crucifixes. I go around to the passenger side of the van, musing about how ugly it is when I see the words:

SO IS YOUR FACE

spray-painted in black on the sliding, side door. I laugh, immediately getting the joke, but then realize that if anyone in Beckett drove a van like this, they'd have a rock thrown through their windshield.

"Don't you get flak from people?" I ask Jeff, brushing a McDonald's french fry off the bench seat before adjusting my feet among the fast food wrappers and beer cans that litter the floor.

"Do I get flak?" Jeff furrows his brows as he starts the engine.

"I mean, don't you get pulled over, driving around in this thing?"

"The cops know me here." He shrugs, flipping on the radio. "As far as what other people think? I don't give a rat's ass—"

"Leave it here," Stan demands as Blondie's, "Heart of Glass" crackles over the airwaves.

Jeff lifts his ass and farts. I clap a hand over my nose. The smell is worse than the Piska River in summer.

Jeff smirks at me in his rearview mirror. "You'll have to get used to my farts, Gina. Everyone else has—"

"Jeff, I will never get used to your farts. I can smell the cheeseburger you ate last night." Danny cracks his window.

"Then stop pulling my finger," Jeff snorts.

Ignoring everyone around him, Stan rocks out to Blondie, his head moving in semi circles like the blue rabbit's foot—hanging from Jeff's rearview—does, every time the van makes a turn.

"Where'd you learn to play like that?" Jeff asks me, his tone neither supportive nor jeering.

"Um...listening to my favorite records...playing by ear, I guess."

"What're your favorite groups?"

Jeff looks unimpressed when I rattle off my list.

"Wanna jam sometime?"

"I, uh…wow, I'd love—"

"I'm just inviting you to jam. I'm not asking you to join the band." Amusement flashes in his eyes when they meet mine in the rearview.

"Oh, well, I didn't think, um…I know." My cheeks burn.

"Where am I taking you?"

"42nd...?" It's the only street name I can think of.

"42nd?" Jeff scrunches his nose.

I clear my throat. "Yeah."

****

"Right here's good," I tell Jeff, pointing to a restaurant called Sardis. The place is well lit with lots of people inside, the warm glow of its windows a beacon among the damp, dark street filled with X-rated theaters and hookers.

I take my time gathering my stuff, wet from earlier. The rain is letting up. Mist shimmers in a blend of colors on Jeff's windshield from the neon lights. But the night air feels damper than it had when it was raining. Danny looks a little worried as I climb out. He and Jeff exchange glances. Stan continues to bop to the radio, not once turning around. This saddens me.

"Drop by the studio sometime if you wanna jam," says Jeff.

Danny gives me a goofy grin. "Be safe, Gina...."

The sliding door bangs shut. The tires squeal as Jeff speeds off. I draw in a shuddering breath, watching the van's tail lights reflect on the wet pavement and then vanish among the steam rising from the manhole covers.

****

At first I don't hear Jeff's horn because I'm crunching on toffee peanuts while watching a steel pan drummer busk for change on the corner. When I hear my name, I look up and see a crown of fiery hair poking out of the window of an ugly Dodge van, from the other side of 42nd Street. "We're having a little party at Joni's. Get in the van," Jeff shouts.

****

"No shoes in the house. That's the rule," Joni says, not batting an eye when she sees me enter the kitchen with the boys. Her house smells vaguely of pot roast, which makes my stomach growl.

My loafers are wet and grimy from the streets, and I wonder how I might get them off without anybody knowing how bad my feet smell. As it is, a street-like stench clings to my soggy windbreaker. I catch Joni studying me from the corner of her eye as she empties packets of Carnation instant cocoa mix into a set of coffee mugs.

"Gina, you're welcome to use the shower. I'll get you a change of clothes."

"Oh...." My face blooms hot as I gaze down at my wet socks.

"Don't feel bad, Gina. We've all been there." Joni puts a kettle on for hot water, then leads me to a door down the hall. It opens on to an oversized bathroom. "There's towels in the closet. Help yourself."

The daisies on the shower curtains, which wrap around the jacuzzi-style tub, blur with my tears. Joni's voice can be heard on the other side of the door and down the hall. I can't pluck out her words, but I can hear her laughing with the boys over music by The Replacements, playing softly on the stereo.

I feel weird about undressing in some strange bathroom, and not just a strange one but a nice one, with two sinks and bronze drying racks, strung with matching towels. And I wonder, as I avoid stepping on the plush, white bathmat, so as not to pollute it with my grubby feet before setting foot in the tub, how it is I've turned into such a crybaby. I never remember having bawled this much as a kid. Once, during music lessons at school, I started bawling for no good reason. I tried to apologize to Mr. Barton but he told me not to worry, that it was hormones, that it was a teenager thing.

Elaine has refused to talk about hormones. Whenever I'd ask her questions about my body changing, she'd get this panicked look and then mumble something like, 'Don't ask me, Gina. I don't know these things.' Once, when I told her that sometimes I feel sad for no good reason, all she said was, 'You're moody like Ellen was. Don't worry, babe. It runs in the family.'

What family?

****

The gang is lounged around the living room, talking and sipping cocoa from their mugs. Joni lies on the floor, her head in Stan's lap, her feet in Jeff's. Danny sits indian style at the end of the coffee table, flipping a deck of cards. Everyone becomes quiet when I come out, my hair damp and wearing a tight purple sweater and black mini-skirt Joni had given me. The only sound is the music. And all of the sudden it's as if the living room's avocado green walls are much too avocado-like. Maybe I'm hanging out inside of an avocado.

"So Gina, what's your deal?" Jeff asks, massaging Joni's feet between sips of cocoa.

"My deal?" I feel like I'm auditioning for a part in a play or something, standing there like a dumbass in the middle of the living room.

"How'd you end up in the city?"

"Do I have to talk about this...now?" I catch Stan from the corner of my eye. He's staring into space. Joni's staring lazily up at me.

"We wanna know who we're partying with."

"My aunt's a drunk and the most irresponsible person I've ever known. According to her, I'm a waste of space, so I left," I say to the floor, hoping they won't press me for any more details.

Pause.

"Your dad?"

"Don't know the guy."

"Mom?"

"Dead."

"Oh." Jeff shrugs.

Danny looks hangdog. "Gee...."

Stan and Joni say nothing.

"Sorry," Jeff says.

I wait for the others to share their stories. Nobody offers a thing.

"So, what's the surprise?" Jeff taps Joni on the sole of her foot.

She rolls to a seated position, nods her chin at the Danish Butter Cookie tin, on the glass coffee table.

They go from smoking pot to sipping cocoa and eating cookies? Seems like the party already happened, at the rehearsal space.

"That's crazzzy," Danny laughs when Joni opens the

tin.

There are Brach's individually wrapped hard mints inside. Maybe two dozen of them. So what? I get them in my Christmas stocking every year with a juicy, Florida orange. I hate them. I associate them with bad breath or something you get with the bill at a restaurant.

"Gina doesn't get it," Jeff laughs, moving to the overstuffed, leather couch.

"What don't I get?" I snap. All I want to do is sleep.

"Don't get your panties in a knot." He slides the bean bag chair toward me, with his foot. "Take a load off."

"These candies are dosed, Gina," Joni says, lighting a vanilla incense cone.

My eyes linger on hers, waiting for her to fill me in, but she switches off the floor lamp, then moves to the other side of the coffee table to squeeze in next to Jeff, who watches me as I plop down in the bean bag chair.

"Have you tripped before?" she asks.

"No," Jeff volunteers.

"You don't have to answer for me. I got vocal chords." I glare, fiddling with the loose thread on the end of Joni's sweater.

"We'll go easy on you." Joni smirks. "They're fairly mild...if you eat just one."

"Mind if we eat more than one?" says Stan.

"Eat however many you want. I don't need all this."

"You better not let Janis get her hands on 'em," Danny says.

"Why not? An acid trip might make my little sister grow up a little," says Joni.

Stan chews five mints at once. Jeff grabs five. He crunches the first four. Upon unwrapping the fifth, he pauses, then drops it back in the tin. Joni eats three. Danny chews two more—no sucking, no taking it slow. They leave a pile of cellophane wrappers on the glass coffee table.

"You don't have to," Joni tells me.

"Uh, I will…in a minute." All eyes are on me as I set my mint down on the table.

"Eat it or put it back."

Taken aback by Jeff's abruptness, I drop my mint in the tin, knowing nothing about acid except the occasional rumor about some guy jumping out a window because he thinks he can fly, or the girl going blind from staring at the sun. I've always wondered how much was true and how much was a load of shit.

The stoner crowd at Chatswick would always hang out on the smokers' bench before first period and brag about how they tripped over the weekend. I've heard them describe the experience as indescribable. Some said they saw colors and things melting. Others said they had conversations with people that weren't even there. One girl said she'd had a conversation with the funny look-ing dude on the cover of Mad Magazine. It all sounded like a bunch of science fiction to me. Still, the stoner kids seemed perfectly normal to me—no crossed eyes or drooling or anything.

"Going out for a butt." Joni gets up. She heads for the patio. Jeff and Stan follow.

"Are you okay, Gina?" Danny sits next to me while I slouch in the bean bag, my knees pressed together, so I won't flash anybody.

"I don't know...is acid the same thing as LSD?"

Danny giggles. I frown. He's the last person I would expect to laugh at me.

"Sorry." He claps a chubby hand over his mouth. "Yes, it is...maybe you should try it...might put you in a better mood."

"I'm not in a bad mood."

"Okay, I didn't mean it like that. I meant that if you take one, you might stop taking life so serious-ly or..." He scratches his chin, raising a brow as he says this. "You might take life more seriously—it could go either way. You gonna trip or what?"

I crane my head toward the living room arch-way. Beyond the dining room, beyond the sliding glass door that leads to the patio, the others are smoking. Stan's arms are wrapped around Joni's waist and he is swinging her around. Jeff leans against the picnic table, doubled over with laugh-ter.

I inspect one of the mints, wrapped in cello-phane, finding it creepy that there's nothing un-usual in the way it looks. I note, as its sweet, minty hardness crunches under my molars, that there's nothing unusual about its flavor either.

"I'm here if things get too intense for you," Danny says.

When forty minutes pass and I don't feel a thing, I start to think, with disappoint and relief, that my sucker is a dud. I head for the patio to smoke. The night has cleared. A cluster of stars twinkle over the tree line that divides Joni's lawn from her neighbor's. We're in some suburb, north of the Bronx.

My teeth won't stop clenching. At first, I blame this on the cold patio chair, which penetrates the thin material of the skirt I'm wearing. But then my whole jaw feels tense and my spit tastes vaguely like metal.

Joni steps outside. She flips the collar on her leather jacket to block the wind as she lights a smoke. She seems small and far away, even though she's within arm's length. "Where you from?" She asks, exhaling smoke.

It takes a moment for me to understand the question, as if it'd traveled many miles to reach my ears. "Up-state...."

"Here, in Northern Westchester?"

"Northern Westchester...?" I scrunch my nose, shaking my head as I do. My shoulders feel like cement.

"S'okay...you don't have to tell me...."

"Beckett...."

"Beckett?"

The name Beckett sounds strange when Joni repeats it.

"Yeah, Beckett...."

"Where's that?"

"The foothills...." I shiver again, but the shiver isn't from the cold. It seems to be coming from somewhere deep inside of me. My stomach is starting to feel weird, too.

"That near Buffalo?" Joni drags from her cigarette, then tosses it into the ash can. Her arm suddenly becomes eight arms. The cigarette makes a comet trail on its way to the can, a comet trail with bird wings....

"Wings," I mutter.

"Huh?"

"Buffalo wings."

Joni busts up laughing. "How'd we end up on the subject of chicken?"

I have no idea, I only know my scalp muscles feel like they're seizing up and my breathing sounds way too loud. It fills my ears. The patio light grows dim.

"Gina, you're priceless." Joni catches her breath. She stops laughing. She scans me with her eyes. "I really like your hair."

"You do?" I'm shocked by the weightlessness of her touch as she combs a hand through my hair and I shiver. I'd forgotten all about my Rod Stewart haircut, but am surprised by how wispy I feel—like smoke swirling in the treetops.

"My aunt cut it...." The thought of Elaine gives me a heavy feeling in my stomach and I suddenly wonder what she might be up to just now. Is she panicking over me? Is she out of her mind with worry? Or is she glad to have me out of the way?

"Why're you holding your stomach?" Joni stops touching my hair. Her hand drops in her lap.

"It feels really strange."

"Oh. You took a hit?"

"Huh?"

"Is it kicking in?'

"I guess. Am I supposed to feel like this?"

"Your stomach might feel gross at first, but once the stuff really kicks in it'll be fun and you won't really notice." Her voice sounds echoed and far away. "But don't think about negative stuff or it'll ruin your trip. That's the trick to avoiding bummers."

"Bummers?"

"Bad acid trips."

"Oh."

"Mind over matter. That kind of thing."

"Right...." Whoa. At first I only think that my eyes are playing tricks on me, but when I look at my hands, the skin starts to bubble—well, not bubble exactly, but ripple. I turn my gaze on the patio. Its smooth, gray surface becomes a galaxy of swirling, shifting patterns that swell and then shrink. One minute they're green and orange flames, the next they're flowers, but if I stare longer they're paisley prints. When I blink, they all disappear and I see just a patio, for a second, before my eyes goof on me again. I could stare at the patio all night.

"Are you peaking?" Joni smiles.

"I think I'm fucked up," I giggle. The chilled night fills my lungs until they feel like hot air balloons. I begin rubbing my knees. These sensations might be an illusion, but the need to go in and get warm is real. Besides, there's a whole frontier like Joni's living room waiting for me to rediscover it. I quickly forget about Elaine.

"I'm frozen," I announce, standing up, as if the threat of hypothermia is a brand new discovery for me.

We wander inside. Devo booms from the speakers. The band is an assault on my ears after having been on the quiet patio. I totter along the plush, beige carpeting, feeling its fibers shift under my feet. The sensation reminds me of the time I'd stood on the beach feeling the wet sand wash out from under my feet whenever the waves rolled in.

Jeff giggles and the carpet starts to breathe. It rolls like waves. I close my eyes and imagine I'm on a raft floating out to sea. When I open my eyes, Jeff's hair is melting and his face looks terrifyingly beautiful, and funny at the same time. He is beautiful, and I want to tell everyone how beautiful everything is—but all I can do is laugh.

The vanilla incense fills my nostrils, and the shadows, cast by the house plants, vibrate on the ceiling. They're so awesome to watch I can barely stand it, and just as I'm about to lose my cool, I turn my attention to my skirt. The fake material looks three-D, like I can reach in and pluck out each individual fiber with my fingers. From the other side of the room, Joni starts to breath way too loud and I want to tell her to stop, but all I can do is laugh. She's talking to Stan about something really deep, I can tell by the look on her face but I can't follow the conversation because their voices sound like fifty people whispering at once. They stop. Joni looks at Danny who is on all fours, staring into the carpet.

"Danny, what're you doing?" she asks.

"I'm looking for my car." He looks up, his expression wild.

Jeff bursts out laughing.

I become confused and upset, because laughing at Danny is the cruelest thing in the world. Jeff's eyes become two black buttons, making him look like a demented Raggedy Ann doll. Joni and Stan laugh too, flashing their teeth, which look like Bugs Bunny teeth.

Danny joins them, his laugh filling the room, and I become even more confused—but at least Jeff no longer looks like a Raggedy Ann doll—and I quickly forget what it is that had me riled—but now the smell of soil from the potted plants begins to turn my stomach, so I venture toward the coffee table, fascinated by the SWISH SHWASH sounds my knees make on the carpet.

"It's a great rug for tripping," Joni agrees with me. "How're you doing over there, Danny? Did you find your car?"

Danny lies on his back, gazing at the ceiling. "No...I lost it...but then, I lost it a long time ago. But I did just find myself."

"Where? In the carpet?" asks Jeff.

"No. In the back seat of my car, which I can't find."

"Danny, you don't have a car," Joni says.

"I did when I lost my virginity in the back seat...what're we talking about?" Danny giggles. "Gina, do you know what we were talking about?"

I don't, but this really cool thought comes to me, but then slips away before I can put it in words. I wriggle closer to Stan. His pupils are huge. Slivers of blue frost are all I can see of his irises.

"Going for a smoke." Jeff gets up. Joni and Danny follow.

"Aren't you going outside?" I ask Stan, glad I'm still capable of small talk.

He shakes his head and his face suddenly changes. The muscles surface from under his skin, then the veins, then the arteries, until it all melts away and all I can see is his skull. When I blink, he's back to normal and leaning back on his hands, his face cocked toward the ceiling, exposing his neck.

I lean in, giving him a peck on that fleshy area of his neck. He grins, looks at me, but doesn't move. When I kiss his Adam's apple, he grabs my hand and I start to pull away, but then let my arm go slack. A warmth bleeds through me as he kisses the inside of my wrist and then, one by one, takes my fingers into his mouth. The rough, wet texture of his tongue sends shivers through my body and I don't want him to stop—but then I hear footsteps creak through the kitchen.

Stan pulls away when a girl, looking like a younger version of Joni, enters the living room, then makes a beeline for the bathroom.

"We'll pick up where we left off," Stan whispers in my ear.

"Do you think...?"

"Janis knows we do acid all the time."

They do this all the time? I remember Joni

saying that the acid was mild. She calls this mild?

Janis comes out of the bathroom. She pauses in the archway, her eyes darting about as she toys with her ponytail. She grins at Stan, and blushing asks, "Where's Joni?"

"Outside...how's school?"

"It stinks." She flips her ponytail over her shoulder.

"Joni tell you she's moving into her art studio?"

"No, but I heard. Mom's not happy about it."

"But, it's within walking distance of the hottest art galleries. It'll be good for her."

"Mom doesn't think so. She reads the paper. She thinks there's too many drugs down there in the city...and Joni just got off probation." Janis' full lips are drawn in a pout. She avoids making eye contact.

"You gonna be bummed when she leaves?"

"Not really. All she and Mom do is fight...although once she's gone, all Mom's focus is gonna be on me...I know this from those two times Mom had kicked Joni out. Once Joni wasn't around to nag, she'd gotten all over my case instead, even though I made the honor roll."

The others return from the patio. Crisp, winter air wafts from their coats as they flop down on the couch.

"What're you doing, having a party?" Janis asks.

"Something like that," says Joni. "This is Gina. She just moved here."

Janis plunks herself down in the bean bag chair. Her eyes are wide and doe-like, yet they all of a sudden seem much too big for her face. I begin to shiver as she morphs into Chaz, the scrawny kid with the poached egg eyes.

"How do you like it here?"

"Uh...." A wave of nausea sets in.

"You must be desperate to hang around with losers like my sister," she says in a voice that sounds much too slow.

"What?"

"What?"

"What'd you say?" The room becomes a mad swirl of red and violet.

"I said, you must be desperate to hang out with losers like my sister. I was joking," Janis assures, even though the look in her eyes tells me different.

"Joking?"

"Joking."

You shouldn't've been there in the first place. You deserve what you get....

Janis' eyes suddenly look like Elaine's when she drinks: big and bloodshot. I then become confused as to why I'm here and how I got here. My pulse rushes to my fingertips and my heart slams in my chest so hard, I'm sure everyone in the room can hear it—maybe everyone in town can hear it.

"You okay, Gina?" Danny's eyes look bizarre and bulbous.

'Don't think about negative stuff or it'll ruin your trip,' Joni'd said. I look to her, but she's chatting with Jeff and is oblivious to my noisy heartbeats.

"Gina, you look flush. Are you sure you're okay?" Danny's eyes suddenly grow small, like pig's eyes.

"I…I'm not sure." I press my hands palm down on the coffee table, appreciating the coolness of its glass surface. Suddenly, I find the fact that I'm not sure amusing and burst out laughing. A ball of colorful patterns explodes across the wall. Everyone, except Janis, laughs with me. My pulse slows.

"You guys are on something, aren't you?" Janis, now looking like Janis, looks from me to Joni, her eyes showing disgust.

"We're on Brach's Peppermints." Joni narrows her eyes at Janis.

"Let me guess...you put something in them?" Janis crosses her arms.

"No...no...I didn't put anything in them." Joni smirks, shaking her head.

"I meant, they have something in them, don't they?"

"Correct. Congratulations, Brains."

"That drug will rot your mind."

"How do you know? Ever try it?"

"No. I like my brain cells."

"You're a hypocrite."

"Am not!"

"You drink."

"Alcohol is legal—"

"You puked at our cousin's wedding from drinking all that champagne."

"I only had one glass. I got sick from the wedding cake...and it was hot," Janis huffs, sinking lower in the bean bag chair. "Your eyes look funny. Hope you sober up by the time Mom gets in."

"We won't be down from this stuff for a couple of days," Stan laughs.

I inspect my hair in Joni's bathroom mirror, not understanding what it is she sees in it—not that it matters, since no one in the city cares what you look like. People in this town, wherever it is we are, care quite a bit, however.

On the way here, Jeff stopped at a 7-Eleven. Me and Stan went in to get a cherry Slurpee. While waiting in line to pay, this fat-necked kid, sporting a baseball cap on backwards began grumbling to the cashier about 'all the freaks who seem to be multiplying in his town.' He then growled, 'Fucking queer!' at Stan, as we were leaving. Stan ignored him, but when we got outside, he walked up to the only other vehicle in the lot—a red Ford pickup with a New York Yankees bumper sticker—and with a black marker, drew a giant penis and balls on the hood of the truck. Below, he wrote:

THANKS, THE SEX WAS FABULOUS!

I grin, remembering the incident, until a corpse grins back at me in the mirror. A wave of stars explode behind my lids when I close my eyes. My face returns to normal when I open them.

In the hallway, I become disoriented, and it takes a minute to find the living room, which seems to have shrunk. Everyone but Janis has left. She's on the couch crocheting. Danny is out-side laying on the picnic table.

Down the hall I hear Joni laugh and say, "Stop

it! You're gonna make me sick!" The door on the end is open a crack. She and Stan and Jeff are on the water bed. Jeff is on all fours making waves. He looks up at me. "We thought you drowned in the toilet."

Joni stops laughing. She and Stan are laying on their backs, their heads propped on pillows. I linger in the doorway, feeling like I've walked in on something. Judging from the scatter of family photos, including one very old black and white one of a woman in a wedding dress, mounted next to the crucifix above the bed, I am guessing this is the parents' bedroom.

"Get on the bed." Jeff flops down on Joni's other side, making really big waves on purpose.

"It's even heated." Joni punches Jeff's shoulder.

"There's not enough room." I note that the bed seems small for even three people, although hanging out in the living room, trying to hold a hopeless conversation with a kid sister who doesn't approve of drugs, or freezing my ass off on the patio with Danny, doesn't seem like an option.

"Here, Gina." Stan moves closer to the wall.

The waves cause me to lurch forward as I squeeze in between Stan and Joni. I get a little freaked by the gurgling sounds the bed makes. The four of us grow quiet as we lie gazing at the ceiling. The smell of shampoo from Joni's hair overwhelms me. But I lie there, stiff as an ironing board, my hands tucked at my sides—as if it matters, since we're so squeezed in our shoulders touch and I can feel the sweat from Stan's body. His face is tilted toward mine. His breath tickles my cheek and I shiver. In response, a wave of blue, swirling patterns spread along the ceiling's drop down panels.

Stan's hand brushes mine and before I know it, we're holding hands. The smoothness of his palm makes me lightheaded, and the swirling blue patterns become green and orange zig-zagging lines.

"Don't!" Joni hisses, elbowing Jeff. The waves rock violently.

"My God, what was that?" Jeff mocks surprise.

"You, and you goosed me, you dink."

"No, I didn't."

"Did you goose her?" Stan asks.

"Dude, I didn't touch her," Jeff laughs.

The bed lurches as Joni and Jeff wrestle but then start to make out. Jeff rolls onto Joni's other side, next to me, and I end up with some of his hair in my mouth.

Waves rock the bed as I try to scoot over but am mashed against Stan who hooks an arm around my waist. I find myself cocooned in his warmth and welcome it, except...he's starting to grind against me. The stoner girls at Chatswick call it 'dry humping'. Not sure I'm into dry humping or not, I lie very still, on my side, facing Joni as Stan's hand roams up the back of my blouse. The room glows violet, then red as he unhooks my bra.

Joni is straddling Jeff. She's unzipping his jeans. She notices me watching her. "Join us, Gina."

Before I can understand what's happening, she plants a kiss on my mouth. Her lips are soft and taste like bubblegum lip gloss. I don't resist but I don't exactly kiss her back, either.

"You look totally freaked. Relax, girl." She rolls onto the bed and strokes my hair.

Maybe I ought to trust them? After all, they've taken me under their wings....

Part of me feels ashamed when I let Joni touch me, like what we're doing is wrong—even though part of me feels extremely turned on. Stan starts to French kiss Joni, while Joni runs a hand up my skirt and Jeff touches my boobs....

I begin to feel pretty wet down there but a little scared, too. There are too many hands on too many places, and too many legs and too many tongues. When someone tries to pull my underwear down, I panic.

There's a knock on the door and everyone freezes. Thank God. The door swings open.

"What're you doing in Mom's room?" Janis looks dumbfounded and frightened, which makes me feel ashamed. I wonder how long she'd been lingering outside the door.

"I didn't say you could come in!" Joni barks, her face twisted in fury. She peels herself off me so fast, she nearly tumbles off the bed, her boobs bouncing in the movement.

"Mom's home." Janis backs away.

"Shit. Okay." She shuts the door in Janis' face. She faces me, her eyes wild. "You see Danny?"

"Uh...on the picnic table."

"Hope he's not having a freak out or some stupid shit."

"Let's blow." Jeff fastens his belt. Stan tucks his shirt in his jeans. His bulge is obvious.

"Joni!!!" Joni's mother yells from the kitchen as we trundle into the living room. "What'd I tell you about burning that incense crap in the house?"

"Sorry, Mother. I forgot."

"I can't remember where my shoes are," I whisper, noticing that the stereo is off and the lights back on.

"They're at the door, and you don't have to whisper," says Jeff as we enter the kitchen. Joni's mother is at the sink. She reeks of perfume. Her long, black hair melts into the wallpaper as she washes the cocoa mugs we left in the living room. The cookie tin melts into the kitchen counter top.

"You're supposed to be on a diet, Mother." With a panicked look, Joni swipes the tin off the counter. "You haven't eaten any of these, have you?"

"Of course not. I hate the things. They're something I'd eat only if I thought I had bad breath."

Joni stuffs the tin in her Jansport bag. "We're leaving," she tells Danny, who, having returned from the patio, stands in the middle of the kitchen with a dazed look, leaving the door wide open. "Shut the door."

"Well, I...uh…." Danny giggles.

Joni's mother cranes her neck, looks puzzled for a moment, then suspicious. I can tell, even with the crinkles around those tired eyes, so dark brown that they're almost black, that she'd been really pretty once. She crosses her arms, looking from Danny to Jeff to Stan who smirks and says, "Hi, Mom," giving her a peck on the cheek.

"Hi, Stanley."

"You have a good night at work?" Joni slips on her boots, her eyes avoiding her mother's.

"It's the same every night," she says a little stiffly, grabbing a carton of milk from the fridge. "Where are you headed?"

"Out." Joni shrugs.

"Be careful driving, Jeff. There are a lot of idiots on the road tonight."

"I will," Jeff says, grinning.

My eyes widen with terror when Jeff's nose grows long, then melts away. I clap a hand over my mouth to keep from laughing.

****

"You're gonna drive on this stuff?" I say as we pile into the van.

"Why not? I'm a master at driving on acid." Jeff starts the engine. It grunts and wheezes before spluttering to a heavy idle.

"Jeff always stops for the pink elephants in the cross walk," Stan says. Everyone laughs.

"Where are we going anyway?" says Joni.

Excellent question. Tiny droplets tumble from my mouth as I exhale. My breathing becomes shallow and my teeth clench again, not just from the cold and the acid but because I don't know what comes next. Would they drop me off at 42nd and say, 'See ya around?' Although maybe that'd be for the better....Too many hands on too many places and too many legs and too many tongues

I'm glad Janis walked in on us.

****

In Manhattan, the rest of us stand shivering on the curb while Jeff places a cardboard sign in the rear window of his Dodge:

PLEASE DON'T BREAK INTO ME.
THRERE'S NOTHING
INSIDE ME WORTH STEALING!!!

We're in front of a five story tenement with a bricked over entrance. An iron rail wraps around a rectangular hole in the sidewalk, looking much like a burial plot connected to a set of cement steps that drop below street level. The dim light of the streetlamp casts bar-like shadows on our faces as we slip down the throat of the stairwell, making our way to the basement. At the bottom, Joni and the boys wriggle their way through a narrow gap in a doorway that's mostly bricked over.

"Coming, Gina?" Danny's voice sounds muffled.

I'm still outside the gap, alone and hesitant, my insides turning to jello. The concrete under my feet starts to breath and turn several shades of red and violet. The air outside is raw, yet I feel an icy draft seep from the inside of the building, carrying with it a dank and sour smell—as if the building had been hiding things that haven't seen daylight for a very long time.

Inside, the air is heavy and black as a mine shaft's. In my acid state, the air may as well be made of velvet. I imagine it breaking apart into a million little pieces before shape shifting into millions of swooping bats. The thought causes my lids to flutter...or maybe it's just the dust in the air causing them to flutter. Mildew and rot hits my nostrils and I sneeze six times. I feel like a dust mite trapped in a Hoover vacuum bag.

With just the flashlights to see by, I'm only able to catch glimpses of things: a critter-eaten mattress laying on the dirt floor, cobwebs dripping from a very low ceiling, a mouse darting behind a stack of rotted newspapers and a water-damaged painting of Jesus, which leans against a brick wall, sooty from a fire.

I shuffle behind Danny, keeping my eyes pointed to my feet as I sidestep loose bricks, clutching his sweaty hand as we inch toward the wooden staircase. I hear creaking noises and look up.

A face, whiter than cottage cheese, floats among the shadows, its greenish eyes meeting mine. I scream. Danny drops his flashlight, the face disappears and we're plunged in darkness.

"There's someone in here," I whimper, groping the air, hoping to reconnect with Danny. Instead, my hand brushes the wall and then something hard, flat and glassy. "Where am I?" I whine.

"Hold on, hold on," Danny mutters. There's a shuffling sound and then CLICK, CLICK. A beam of yellow light, choked with dust particles, pierces the dark above, and I make out the hems of Stan's jeans. He and Joni and

Jeff are already halfway up the staircase, which is missing half its steps. Stan points his flashlight toward the floor. The flashlight is at Danny's feet.

"Okay, Stan. Got it," Danny sounds embarrassed. "You okay, Gina? What'd you see?" I realize then, when he shines his flashlight on the wall beside me, that I'd seen my own reflection in the cracked, full-length mirror—the kind you'd find at a Woolworth's—leaning against the wall.

Everyone laughs, including me.

"'Kay, Gina. Hang on to my arm."

Upstairs, I catch more glimpses: windows sealed with brick, mold blooming along baseboards, wallpaper peeling away in huge tongues, carpets stained and rotted. The narrow halls ripple under my feet if I stand still for longer than a second. A breeze, carrying a raw chill, seeps through the windows, stripped of their glass, as we reach the fourth story. Moonlight creeps in at strange angles, splashing in the doorways, refracting in the windows, illuminating the walls choked with graffiti. From my peripherals, shapes and shadows dart along baseboards but vanish whenever I look straight on. Flashlight beams dash along corroded tin ceilings, dance along cracks in the plaster that web their way toward patches of flimsy lath boards.

We reach the top floor. The windows are nailed with plywood. The end of the hall sinks several inches, causing the last door on the right to slope at a funny angle. Jeff works his key in the lock, then gives the door a strong kick. It pops open with a shriek, wobbling drunkenly on its hinges.

I blink in amazement, my eyes almost watering when Stan flips on a fifties style lamp and I find myself in a room with a an indian style rug laid out in front of a saggy velvet couch and a stack of milk crates, housing sci-fi paperbacks.

Slumped in the corner of a makeshift kitchen, is a rust-streaked sink with no handles and a pale of water in its basin. Nailed above, is a plastic apple clock with a bite mark where the three would be. At first, I think it's the acid causing the number eleven to move. When I do a double take, I realize that there's a cockroach hanging out between the two ones. It darts under the minute hand.

Stan reaches for the pellet gun that'd been laying on the card table. He fires it at the cockroach. The pellet hits the clock face, the clock falls and lands with a plop in the bucket of water.

"You're buying me a new one, Jordan." Jeff lights a cigarette.

"Sorry Little Debbie, didn't realize you were so attached to your apple clock."

"Hey, I bought that as a souvenir when I first moved here. The bite mark symbolizes an important move...you know, taking a bite out of the Big Apple, which I gotta admit is biting me back."

Danny offers me a slice of bologna from their styrofoam cooler.

"No thanks, Danny."

He wipes the mouse turds off the counter with a

sponge, then lights the propane cooker. He grabs a can of creamed corn from the shelf. More roaches scatter.

"Where...?" I sit on the edge of a metal, folding chair. "Whose um...house are we in?"

The boys look at each other, puzzled. Danny shrugs. "Nobody's. We just, uh, kind of found this building and took it over. Nobody actually lives here...the homeless from Tompkins Square Park occasionally flop in the vacant rooms, on the first floors, but only during the really cold months and they don't come up here and bother us none...we all sort of live here, except Joni."

Oblivious to all, Joni lay on the couch, reading a dogeared copy of *War of the Worlds.*

"She just stays here a lot...and uh, we don't gotta pay rent. Our friend Crossie taught us how to steal electricity from a passing cable, so we live pretty good."

Joni closes the book, yawns and says, "I'm tired. You all tired?" She looks at me.

Earlier, I was very tired, but am now wide awake from the drugs, and frankly I don't know if Joni's look is my cue to leave or to go to bed with her.

"I'm still tripping my balls off," Stan laughs.

"I'm going to the Niagara Bar to shoot pool," says Danny, mopping up creamed corn with a slice of white bread.

"I could lay down." Jeff grins at Joni. Joni grins back at Jeff and then at Stan, whose eyes lock on hers.

My heart bangs in my chest when she gazes at me. I lower my eyes to the linoleum floor, peeled away like third degree burns on flesh in areas. The fibers of the exposed wood floor begin to ripple, along with the low ceiling. The place feels dungeon-like.

"I should leave so you guys can get some sleep," I say, even though the idea of backtracking through the dark stairwells, and the basement with a cracked Woolworth mirror scares the hell out of me—along with spending another night, sleeping in the doorway of a shoe shop.

"You just got here," Joni says in a taunting voice.

"You're not going back to Times Square. Not at this hour," says Danny. "Why don't you join me for a game of pool? I need a partner."

Thank you, Danny.

****

I'm wide awake at five a.m. The couch is comfortable enough, and with the four deadbolts on the door, I guess I feel safe. The acid high is losing its kick but the sound of mice, rustling in the walls and ceiling, keeps me awake, so do the sounds of Joni getting it on with Stan and Jeff. Joni getting it on with Jeff, I don't mind so much, but her getting it on with Stan kind of bothers me. They're not actually loud. It's not like I have to listen to "Oh God, oh God," like when Elaine and Chuck get it on, but there's whispering and giggling in between steady, bumping sounds, brought on, I suppose, from a headboard hitting the wall. I try to shut it out by squeezing my lids but a kaleidoscope pattern of snowflakes and red, neon dots zip across my vision.

My thoughts wander to Elaine. Is she out drinking with Sharon, or home watching *Knots Landing* with Chuck? Knots Landing is her favorite. I used to jokingly call it Snots Landing until Elaine promised to slap me if I said that one more time.

Surely she'd know that I was missing by now. The Blums would call her, no doubt. No more calls to them, though. Not for a while anyway.

****

When I wake, Stan is in the kitchen sipping coffee at the card table in Spider Man pajama bottoms. His pale, brown nubs for nipples peep from a thin and hairless chest. My eyes scan the defined wiriness of his biceps that keep him from being scrawny, like Chaz. Mascara runs in loops under his eyes as he smokes and reads the paper. I'm happy not to be alone in the building.

"The funnies aren't funny anymore," he says, not looking up. "They used to have some great ones—even the Peanuts Gang sucks now."

"Where're the others?"

"Jeff's doing his delivery route."

"Danny?

"You're up late." He folds the paper.

"I am?"

"Uh-huh. It's noon."

"Oh." With the windows sealed over, and the clock broken, I have no way of knowing the time.

"I gotta get motivated." Stan snubs his cigarette. He stretches, then, drawing his knees to his chest, throws his head back and yawns. He cracks his knuckles, letting his feet drop to the floor.

"Hey, you're a really good guitar player." He looks into my eyes and I blush. His eyes are bluer than the damsel flies that buzz along the banks of the Piska River in summer.

"Thanks." I squirm under his gaze. "Bathroom...?"

"Through the door behind me. Crapper's in the tub." He holds his gaze.

A ceramic toilet tank, tipped on its side, is the only thing left of the toilet. 'The crapper,' as Stan calls the big, plastic bucket, sits in the lime-streaked claw tub, with no claws. I heave a disgusted sigh, then hold my breath before lifting the lid.

I return to the card table, wearing the only outfit that hadn't gotten wet during my trek through the rain. The lime-green turtleneck with matching bellbottoms, its hems barely reaching the tops of my ankles, make me look like Kermit the Frog waiting for the Great Flood.

"Gina, I'm headed to a pawn shop near Rivington. I'll show you this great little thrift store on the way." Stan smiles wryly at my turtle neck. "You can get clothes for—"

"All I have is fifteen dollars."

"You can find stuff for as little as fifty cents."

"What's wrong with my clothes?" I stiffen, even though I know what's wrong with them.

"Suit yourself." He shrugs. "Just trying to help."

****

The mannequin in a striped jersey and pink wig, gazes at me through her blue, sightless eyes. I gaze back at her dumbly.

"What's the matter?" Stan looks amused.

"I thought we were shopping."

"You're shopping. I'm gonna put this thing in hock." Stan holds up a distortion petal. "Meet you in an hour." Before I can say anything else, he crosses the street and enters a barred up shop with a Puerto Rican flag over the door.

Granny's Garage smells vaguely of BO and old things. Billy Holiday and B.B. King records line the back wall, along with 8-tracks of Donny and Marie Osmond and Barry Manilow. The TWO FOR A DOLLAR box overflows with old lady hats and scuffed up boots from an era I've only read about in history books.

The Culture Club blares from a boom box atop of a cracked jewelry case full of clip-on earrings, shot glasses from Atlantic City and mismatched wedding flutes. When I see the fondu pot, stacked against a typewriter, missing its ribbon, I begin to have my doubts, until the bell over the door rings and in struts a woman sporting purple hair.

She zeros in on a row of fake fur coats, their hangers strung high from a water pipe that snakes its way along the low ceiling. I'd been so over-whelmed by the carnival of odds and ends, I failed to notice the clothes. I sidle up to the woman to gawk at the coat selection, keeping my eyes peeled for a comfy sweat shirt, one that says I LOVE NEW YORK instead of SYRACUSE UNIVERSITY. I don't find any.

"Lemme know if ya need something, Doll," The big boobed shop owner in pink spandex says to me in a nasally voice, saying, 'Doll' like DAWL.

The woman with the purple hair nods, indicating a need to try on the cheetah-print coat. Spandex Lady yells, "Cassan-dra!!! Wanna help this laaady?!"

A girl with bleached hair saunters out of the dressing room, cracking her gum and toting a bottle of Windex. She slams the bottle down, then climbs a three-step ladder, her expression bored as she snags the coat off the pipe.

"I'm takin' off for tha daaay," Spandex Lady informs Cassandra and then, touching my elbow says, "You just let my daughter..." she says this like DAWDA, "know if ya need anything love." She then looks at Cassandra and, thrusting a manicured nail at the boom box says, "Change the Goddamned station, will ya? Ya scarin' the customas!"

The daughter rolls her eyes.

"Whatta ya think of this?" Spandex Lady holds up a spiked belt for her daughter to see. It's like the one I'd seen at the mall while Mary and I went shopping for school clothes—or I should say, while Mary was shopping for school clothes. "This thing cawst ten dollas brand new. Surprised ya didn' grab it."

Cassandra shrugs. I snatch the belt off the rack the minute Spandex Lady steps out. Granny's Garage only wants twenty-five cents for it.

On the end of an over-stuffed rack, two mini-skirts catch my eye: one made of black vinyl with zippers going up the sides and one with fake snakeskin, its patterns reminding me of Lenny and Squiggy. The skirts are something Joni would wear—or something that bass-player chic at the club would wear. They're only a dollar apiece, but I can't picture myself wearing something that flashy and—slutty.

The woman with the purple hair sidelong glances me. I shoot her my best bored look, pretending that I shop here all the time, then grab the green suede skirt, one a little less minnie than either the zippered or the snakeskin skirt, and head to the dressing room—really just a mop closet with a bed sheet for a door.

In the mirror, I gaze in disgust at my Kermit the Frog outfit, then look away like a vampire might if he saw a crucifix. Ignoring the zit on my ass, which is whiter than a marshmallow in the crude lighting, I slip out of my tired clothes. They lay in a heap on the carpeted floor.

The suede skirt fits surprisingly well, I realize, when I do a twirl in front of the mirror. It's form fitting, which makes me look like I have hips—although I'll have to be careful when bending over. It's still kind of short.

"Gina?" Stan calls my name from the other side of the sheet. Has an hour passed?

"In here." I slide on a pair of Corduroy bellbottoms.

"How's it going?"

"Good, I guess."

"Can I see?"

"Uh...I guess so." I draw back the sheet.

With a deadpan gaze, Stan shakes his head.

Annoyed, I yank the curtain shut, but as I'm jerking on the zipper, I notice that the bell bottoms' hems are two inches over the ankle.

Stan pokes his head in. "High-waters!!!" He sticks his tongue out at me.

He's looking at the leather jackets when I return to the skirt rack. "Why don't you buy something sexy?" He shouts over his shoulder, "Instead of hiding inside those baggy gym clothes you like to wear?"

I pretend to ignore him even as I return to the fitting room with the two slutty skirts. The snake skin is super tight, especially in the butt, as if the snake pattern had been spray painted on me. It makes me look different, more so than the suede skirt had. It's kind of sexy, but...I feel exposed. It's the same with the vinyl skirt.

"Gina?"

"What?"

Stan pokes his head in.

"Will you step out?" I hiss. "Get out."

Instead of leaving, he walks in, draws the sheet closed and flops down on the stool like this is his house or something.

"What the fuck, Stan."

"What?"

"You can't just barge in here."

"Why not? We're roommates now." He inhales fumes

from a small, red and yellow bottle. "Let me see your skirt."

Sighing, I do a full-turn, my eyes avoiding his as I cross my arms. I feel like a chicken on a rotisserie—on display. When I don't hear any snickering, I begin to worry.

"Well?"

Stan's eyes glow. "You look like a hot little ticket." A smile curls on his lips as he runs a hand along one of the zippers.

"Stan." Feeling my face flush, I turn my back to him.

"What?" he laughs.

The space, small to begin with, suddenly feels much smaller. The heat from his body—his smell—takes over. I want to slip out, but he's blocking the door. Before I can understand what's happening he presses his lips against mine, gently, but firmly.

My body feels hot with excitement but I'm confused, because first I'm the creep of Chatswick who, along with the bearded lady, was always picked last for dodgeball, and now, here I am in New York's Lower East Side and I'm a hot ticket. Besides, didn't he just sleep with Joni?

I jerk away when Stan tries to slip his tongue in my mouth. My head bounces off the wood-paneled wall. I rub the area where I whacked myself.

"What's wrong, Gina?" He grins.

"Nothing. Just wasn't expecting to get fucked in the dressing room," I mutter.

"Who said anything about fucking?"

"Will you keep your voice down?" I hiss, not that it matters since Dexys Midnight Runners blares at top volume. Cassandra hadn't changed the music like her mother had asked.

"Just wanted to kiss you."

"Right."

"You're weird. You act like you've never been kissed." Stan flops down on the stool, his smile fading. I glare back at him, dressing quickly.

I march to the register with the skirts and spiked belt. There's a boy in front of me with more jewelry in his ears than I own. The daughter stares blankly at my Kermit the Frog turtleneck. I half-expect her to sneer at it, but she doesn't. Clearly I'm not in Beckett, but I am in the Lower East Side where people don't give a shit what I wear because they don't give a shit period. But their not giving a shit makes me give a shit in ways that I didn't give a shit before when I was surrounded by people who did give a shit. In Beckett, being a slob made me rebellious. Now, in Manhattan, being a slob just makes me a slob.

While Cassandra rings me in, I select black eye shadow from the top of the jewelry case, noting that Joni wears black eyeshadow. I hand Cassandra my money, but she's looking past me and scowling at Stan who's prancing around in a pink wig and making silly faces in the three-way mirror. Cassandra gestures with a stern finger for him to put the wig back on the mannequin's head. He does, then grinning, goes outside.

He's leaning against a lamp post, smoking, when I step out, but he looks bigger somehow. We stride down the avenue, stinking of urine, garbage and fresh-baked pizza.

"Man, why are you so nervous?" Stan asks as we pass a gutted diner, it's storefront window smashed out, its insides blackened with soot. Chrome stumps are all that are left of its stools.

"I'm not nervous—"

"Back there in the dressing room, you acted like I was gonna hurt you."

"Stan, I barely know you." I barely know Jeff and I barely know Joni. "What do you all want from me?"

"I just wanted a kiss." Stan shoots me a baffled look. "I like you."

"I guess I like you too."

We wander toward a basketball court, among a cluster of brick high rises. An occasional THWAK and nervous RAT-A-TAT-TAT on the pavement echoes as young men toss a basketball around screaming, "Yo!" whenever one of them makes a slam dunk.

A woman in a filthy, tweed coat, with scabs on her face, is out cold on one of the benches. Three fat pigeons peck at a Kentucky fried Chicken box under her bench.

"You wanna sit?" Stan says when we take the bench opposite her.

"No. Why?"

"Thought it'd be nice to chill."

We sit.

"Just trying to help." He stares at the sky, deepening to a steel gray and smelling of rain.

"So, shoving your tongue in my mouth is supposed to help me?"

"Why not?" Stan huffs from the yellow bottle again. He's been doing that since we left the squat. "Don't you like to kiss?"

"I don't want that," I say when Stan passes the bottle to me. "What is it anyway?"

"Rush. Have a toot—"

"No, thanks."

"Works like an aphrodisiac—"

"I'll take your word for it," I say, not sure what an aphrodisiac is.

"Listen, I have something for you." With a shit-eating grin, Stan unbuttons his leather jacket. Underneath, is a weather-beaten leather jacket, like the one Joni wore last night. Stan appearing bulkier hadn't been my imagination. Wide-eyed and slack-jawed, all I can do is stare as he holds it up for me to see.

"Well? Why don't you take it?"

"Stan."

"What?"

"Did you steal that?"

"Yup."

"That's bad."

"No, it's not. You're poor and needed a coat. So there." He drapes the jacket over my shoulders.

"How'd you do it?"

"That ditzy chick working the counter was too busy chatting with that woman with the purple hair to notice what was happening."

I toss my Syracuse sweatshirt aside and slip into the leather jacket. It smells old, old but good. It hangs pleasantly heavy on my frame. It makes me feel different somehow. My right pocket feels bulky. When I unzip it, I discover a long-sleeved, striped jersey.

"I stole that too while you were in the dressing room."

"Wow." I blink in amazement at Stan's craftiness.

"Welcome to your new life, Gina," he says.

Stan snatches my sweatshirt, and, walking over to the sleeping woman, drapes it over her sleeping body. I'm not sure I want my sweatshirt gone forever, but know better than to argue with him. Maybe he is trying to help.

We stand. Stan clasps my hand in his, he gives it a peck, his lips like river stones that've been warmed by the sun. He then pecks me on the forehead and on the cheek before gently leading me away from the basketball court.

****

No one's at the squat when Stan and I return, but it's late and I'm full and I'm happy because Stan bought me pizza on the corner. And now I lay on the couch, pulling the sleeping bag Danny'd given me under my chin. It's terribly cold in the squat, even with the electric heater going.

I wait for Stan to say goodnight, but he sits on the arm of the couch, not moving. The dim lighting, cast by the table lamp, makes it hard for me to see his watery blue irises, but the outline of his jaw warms me all over.

He leans down and kisses my lips. I have no idea what to do, so I run my hands through his hair, greasy and stinking of Aquanet. The animal smell of his under-arms is exciting to me. He crouches down. His breath tickles my neck when he nibbles my ear. All I can do is giggle, even though I'm shaking. He kisses me again, this time longer, as he squeezes in next to me, and I can feel the bulge in his pants as his breathing becomes shallow.

"Don't," I say, when he reaches for my zipper.

He looks at me funny.

"You heard me."

He sighs. "Now I've got blue balls."

"You'll live." I sit up, all the while remembering what Mary told me about blue balls. She told me that if a guy doesn't come, he gets this leaden sensation in his balls.

"Why didn't you stop me sooner? You got me worked up for nothing." Stan jerks away when I try to wipe the sweat from his forehead. "Guess I'll leave you alone."

"Where you going?" I grab his hand as he tries to stand.

"My room. Where else?"

"Uh…can I sleep in there?" I don't want him to change his mind about me.

"Why? So you can get me more excited?"

"What if I change my mind about things?"

"What things?"

"Do I have to actually say it?"

"What're you trying to say, Gina? Just say it."

"Like umm...doing it?"

"Oh, you mean fucking." Stan smiles, grabbing my hands in his.

His room is a war zone. The walls are painted black. The ashtray on the bedside table overflows with cigarette butts. A stack of *Playboy* magazines lay half-buried in a mountain of dirty laundry. The only things offering anything in the way of atmosphere are two posters—one of David Bowie, the other of Iggy and The Stooges, and a blue lava lamp, glowing merrily on the dresser. Its white wax bubbles float and stretch like taffy, casting oblong shadows on the ceiling.

Stan gives his comforter a shake, scratching his head in wonder when a dirty tennis shoe tumbles out of the blankets before falling to the floor with a PLUNK. He undresses quickly.

I'd seen him this morning, strutting around without a shirt on. But now, really seeing his body for the first time, I can't help but notice his 'happy trail,' that tiny strip of hair that runs from a guy's belly button to his crotch. I heard it be called that once in an article out of *Cosmopolitan.* His legs are spindly and hairy, and so different from my smooth ones.

I blush when he pulls off his jeans—he isn't wearing underwear. In the dim lighting, I make out the patch of wiry pubic hair. Having been freed from his jeans, his dick springs into the air. My God, it's huge—bigger than many I've seen in

Chuck's collection of *Hustler* magazines.

Does he name it? I've overheard the boys at Chatswick refer to their thing as Junior or some other stupid name, like it's their pet or something. How'll that thing fit inside me?

"What's wrong?" Stan laughs. "Don't you like him?" Pride curls on his lips. "You gonna get undressed or what?"

I realize, then, that I'm just staring. Stan lies back on the bed, wearing just his tube socks. He's propped on his elbows, his shoulders rolled forward, his dick standing on end like a weather stick.

"Can we shut the lights off?"

Stan hits the bedside light. In the dark, I slowly undress, starting with my socks. The only light now comes from the lava lamp, but I can still see him grinning and staring.

"Will you look the other way?"

Stan covers his eyes as I let my oversized T-shirt fall to the floor. Now, in just my flowered underwear, I sit on the edge of the bed with my arms folded across my boobs. They're so small I don't even need a bra. I just wear one to wear one, so I won't be a freak.

Stan strokes my shoulder with one hand, with the other, he rubs my head. This relaxes me. He gently pries my hands from my chest. We embrace. He pulls me onto the mattress. While lying between my legs, he cradles my head in his hands, stroking my hairline with his thumbs. The bedding is a mess. We're on bare mattress, where the bottom sheet had come loose.

"Part your lips," he says. When I do, he kisses me, this

time using his tongue.

"What?" he says when I shrink from his kiss.

"Gross."

"It's not gross. It's sexy. Haven't you French kissed before?"

"I don't see why people think it's so great." I wipe my mouth on the sheet.

"Come on, Gina. You're no fun." Stan grins, pulling me closer. I can feel his dick, stiff as a flag pole on a January morning, against the thin cotton of my underwear. He runs his tongue along my belly, then my nipples, licking them gently, making them harder than I ever knew they could get. Being that I have big nipples, but not much in the way of actual boob, I'd worried that he would be disappointed, but he doesn't seem to care. Not knowing what else to do, I gaze at him with lidded eyes in an attempt to look sexy.

"Don't," I giggle when he starts to lick me—down there. Mary was right, it feels great but....

"What's wrong?" Even in the dim glow of the lava light, I can see he's baffled.

"I don't know...."

"You don't like it?"

"It feels good, but..." I feel so stupid, like maybe I'm doing something wrong, or that I'm about to do something wrong, yet if I don't go along with it, that too would be wrong. I want Stan to like me—maybe even love me, but....

"Gina, are you a virgin?"

I can hear the smile in Stan's voice.

"No."

"Yes."

"So what?"

"Don't get defensive. I'm glad that's all it is. I was be-ginning to think you were weird."

I roll onto my side and face the wall, pulling the com-forter over my shoulder.

"It's not a big deal. People lose their virginity every day."

"Well, I don't lose my virginity every day." I roll over to face him. "What if your dick doesn't fit inside me?"

Stan howls with laughter. "For God's sake, Gina. Women have babies, don't they?" He says as soon as he can catch his breath.

"It's gonna hurt." I shoot him an annoyed look.

"Maybe at first...I'll go slow." He dabs at the tears in his eyes.

"You will?"

"Sure."

"You'll be gentle?"

"Uh-huh."

"If it hurts or I cry, you'll stop?"

"Yeah...." Stan's dick goes soft.

"Am I the first virgin you slept with?" I prop myself on my elbows.

"No."

"Did she feel the way I do?"

"I guess…don't psychoanalyze everything, Gina. It's a waste of brain juice."

"What about your first time? Is it hard for guys?"

"I don't remember my first time...that was a long time ago...when I was twelve and it was with the babysitter."

"May I?"

"Of course, Gina. Guys love it when a girl touches their cock."

We kneel on the bed facing each other. I switch on the bedside light. I cup his balls. They're like Hostess Snow Balls, pink and soft. I've always wondered how guys deal with having a dangly sack between their legs all the time. He closes his eyes while I run my hand slowly, up and down, watching in amazement at how much bigger he gets all of a sudden, as he had before. I hope he's not expecting a blow job.

"Let's do it. I'm ready." He pulls me onto the bed, his dick like marble against my thigh.

In that moment, Elaine's words come marching in, 'Gina, you don't want to end up pregnant and sleeping on someone's couch.'

"What about birth control?" I pry myself from Stan.

"Oh." He looks at me blankly and then does a half-assed search through his night stand drawer. "I'm out of rubbers."

"Crap," I sigh, disappointed and relieved.

"Guess I'm used to my girlfriends taking care of the birth control part."

"Are you saying I'm immature?" This is so not romantic.

"I'm just used to women with more experience."

"So, now what?" I fold my arms across my chest, ready to say forget it.

"I could withdraw," he says in a voice that

makes it sound like he's making a bank transaction. "Besides, rubbers pinch my dick."

"How will you know when to pull out?"

"A guy always knows when he's gonna come."

"This is getting complicated."

"I won't get you pregnant," he whispers in my ear, kissing me again.

We lay back. He guides his dick back to that secret place. I feel the first few inches and cringe.

"You have to relax or I can't get it in all the way."

"Okay." I breath deep while remembering my favorite cloud gazing spot, under this old maple tree in Beckett.

"Good girl," he whispers, giving a thrust.

I suck in my breath and moan. He pulls out halfway, then pushes again and I feel like I'm being reamed in two. Sucking in my breath, I push Stan off of me. He flops down beside me, his dick standing straight in the air.

"You're too big."

"You have to relax—"

"I'm trying," my voice trembles. I'm going to lose him, I just know it. Right now, I think I can understand where Mary's at when it comes to Steve. It's like you gotta keep your guy by keeping up with him.

"I've got something that'll help." Stan pulls a film can from his night stand drawer. He dumps a pill in my palm.

"What's this?"

"Some kind of painkiller...."

"What if I take it and never wake up?" I almost long to go back to the days when guys thought I was creepy, not because I enjoy being thought of as a creep, but because life seemed easier then—more predictable.

"One pill won't put you in a coma. Besides, they're not real drugs. They're a prescription and doctors give them out all the time."

"What're you doing with prescription pills?"

"Uh...these I got from someone who sells 'em over the counter at a twenty-four-hour bodega, in the Bowery."

"Oh." I look at Stan blankly. "Why do you have 'em?"

"I just told you why."

"I know, but why do you take them?"

"'Cause I fucking feel like it. 'Cause I like to get high." Stan sighs. He turns on the lamp, then the stereo. "Why do you gotta ask all these analytical questions?"

"Sorry." I gaze down at the camouflage comforter, half-listening to "Chain Gang" by the Pretenders, warble from the speaker.

"The pills help me sleep," Stan's tone softens. He suddenly looks sad.

"What're they like?" I scoot closer to him.

He looks thoughtful. "They're like being drunk... kind of. You're spacey but relaxed. They make you feel warm and good all over—"

"I change my mind...only one, though."

"I won't let you take more than one."

The idea that Stan won't let me do anything dangerous, makes me feel like I can trust him. The pill is white and has the number 8 on it. Before I can change my mind, I toss it on the back of my tongue. I'm shocked when he swallows six. He shuts off the radio and turns on the TV.

****

My brain feels like my feet do when they fall asleep from having sat in a weird position for too long. My thoughts drift to a place not quite inside my own consciousness yet inside of it at the same time. It's like my head feels unattached to the rest of my body or something.

The sensation reminds me of the time I'd had encephalitis. I'd been five-years-old and Elaine and me were living with her friend Ruthie at the time. Having run a really high fever, I'd become confused and extremely tired. My body felt like an anchor nailed to the ocean floor, while my head felt lighter than the air.

'Where in hell have you been, Elaine? You don't go out partying with your friends when Gina's sick!' I remember Ruthie yelling at Elaine in the hallway of her one level house, her voice sounding garbled like she was talking under water. I remember Elaine entering Ruthie's room where I'd lain—Elaine and I didn't have a room of our own and were sleeping in Ruthie's living room on a foldaway bed.

All I could see of Elaine was her silhouette. She smelled of cigarettes, wine and perfume. I wanted to tell her to tug the chain to the ceiling fan because my head was getting too close to its blade, but I'd become too weak to talk.

I remember my head joining the rest of my body the moment Elaine placed a cool hand on mine. 'Gina, sweetie, I'm gonna take you to the hospital, and you'll feel better fast….'

I wake to an antacid commercial, Stan's cool hand on mine, his silhouette framed in the dim lighting. How long had I been asleep? Did I fall asleep? Or was I so relaxed I thought I'd fallen asleep but was actually awake?

My tongue feels thick and my mouth cottony. My body feels like a sack of grain as I struggle to get at the glass of water on the night stand. Though lukewarm, the water feels good going down. I collapse back on the mattress, feeling incredibly relaxed. Stan cups my boob. It feels good, some-how better than it had before.

"How're you feeling?" He grins lazily.

All I can do is smile. My lips feel too heavy for words, so I close my eyes.

"Feel good?" He props his elbow on the pillow while continuing to touch my body with his other hand.

"Mmm...I just had the craziest dream…or… maybe it was a vision…."

"Hmm…." He takes my fingers in his mouth. The steamy heat of his saliva gives me goose bumps. Forcing my eyes open, I give him a puz-zled look.

"Fingers are an erogenous zone," he tells me.
"Oh...."

We kiss. My hand feels like silly putty as I guide his dick between my legs. The wetness down there and the drowsy effects of the pill allow him to glide past. It still hurts at first, but then I start to feel something like pleasure, but then my mind wanders and he begins to rub my insides raw. It's like having sex with a nail file. While waiting for him to come, which takes forever, I focus on the ceiling.

He cups my ass, suddenly, pumping faster and harder. Some of his sweat drips on me, while I barely crack a sweat. When the bed squeaks, I giggle, hoping the others won't hear us.

When a cry escapes him, I suddenly feel jealous. He's having this mystical experience while I'm only having sex. Does Mary feel this way with Steve?

He pulls out and I flinch when a warm and sticky puddle hits my belly.

"Sorry," he cleans me off with his sheet. Then, with a glow in his eyes, he kisses my cheek. "Thank you so much, Gina."

I look at him strangely. Does he think I'm doing him a favor?

"Thank you for making me feel good. That was nice...." He suddenly looks worried. "Was it any good for you?"

"Sure." I force a grin thinking that it wasn't exactly a scene from a harlequin novel— and it certainly wasn't how Mary described her experience. Maybe there's something wrong with me or...I don't know, maybe just having Stan's love, his acceptance is good enough—that and I finally got over the losing my virginity thing. In the TV's flickering light, I can see blood on the sheet. Not a lot, just a few drops. I'd heard somewhere that that's supposed to happen when a girl gets her cherry popped.

I want to stay up and talk to Stan some more, but he's already asleep. Leaning into his shoulder, I listen to the ticking of the bedside clock until I too fall asleep.

Part Three

The morning is bitter. It stings my nose during my walk to the phone booth. I squint at all the whiteness. The newness. Snow came last night. Not a lot, just a dusting. But it shimmers off the concrete.

I wonder what happened to the phone booth. It has a hole in its glass about the size of a fist and a hairline crack that veins its way toward a bloody hand print. A needle, similar to the kind Mrs. Blum uses for her diabetes, lies on the ground—I've been seeing the things everywhere: in public toilets, under park benches, storm drains....

I step around the needle, then pull the sleeve of my jersey over my hand in order to lift the ear piece off the cradle without touching it. It looks sticky. The phone has a dial tone. For this, I'm glad, since it's the only phone around here that works.

The lemon yellow sunlight, streaming through the glass, burns my eyes as I drop ten cents into the slot before punching Elaine's number, on the greasy keypad, my heart thudding in my chest.

"Gina?"

"Hi, Elaine." I'm surprised when she answers on the first ring, like she'd been expecting my call. Her breathing sounds heavy—or maybe it's my own breathing that sounds heavy. A buzzing sound cuts in.

"Elaine, are you there?"

"Where are you, Gina? Our connection's full of static."

"I'm, uh, in the Lower East Side—"

"Where?" Her voice sounds muffled but surprisingly sober, although it is only nine a.m.

"I'm living in this really cool abandoned building with this band...they let me jam with them sometimes...Stan, the bass player...he really loves me—"

"I can barely hear you, Gina. Hang on."

For a moment I hear nothing except buzzing, which grows louder, until I'm sure I've lost her. My fingers are numb from gripping the steel cord of the receiver. A biting wind cuts through, sending copies of the *New York Daily News* and pigeon feathers dipping and weaving across the filthy pavement. A black Trans Am with tinted windows speeds past. The swoosh of air from its force rocks the booth slightly.

"Where are you?" Elaine's voice comes back. The buzzing has stopped.

"I'm in Manhattan. I met these really great guys...I'm totally making it...things are coming together for me—"

"You sound drunk."

Stan and I got high about an hour ago, by crushing pills and snorting them. It's become our morning ritual. It's interesting that I should sound drunk to Elaine when my voice sounds normal to me.

"Tell me where you are, Gina."

"I told you—"

"Come home. The December issue of *Guitar World* is waiting for you on the table...I take it you found the guitar strings?"

"Yeah, they've gotten their use. Been making money in the subway, playing guitar. I'm doing it, Elaine. I'm building a life for myself—"

"Gina, you belong—"

"I hate Beckett—"

"Things weren't as bad as you're making them out to be—"

"Yeah? What about on Labor Day when you were so drunk, you passed out in the middle of the traffic median between the IGA and the gas station?"

"I don't remember that—"

"Of course you don't."

A long pause. For a moment all I hear is her breathing on the other end, and salsa music, drifting from the twenty-four-hour convenience store, next door.

"It'll be Christmas soon," Elaine says, finally.

"Uh-huh."

"You'll be home, then." She makes it sound like I'm vacationing somewhere and that I'll be back soon.

"I'm not coming home."

"I'm working Friday nights again, for extra money. So now I can treat you to dinner at Happy Fridays...we can even go to the salon and you can get your hair cut all cute like you like it...I realize you don't like me touching your hair—"

"I'm not coming home."

"I'll Western Union you some money and you can buy a bus ticket home...better yet, tell me where you are and I'll come get you—"

"I'm not coming home." I start to shake all over

as a tear slides to the end of my nose.

"We used to be such a tight little unit, you and me."

"Yeah, when I was like three-years-old—"

"Why are you doing this?"

"You never once told me you loved me. Maybe I'm only a niece and not your daughter, but don't you know I need to hear 'I love you' once in a while?"

An even longer silence follows. An old woman, sporting a heavy parka, trundles past with a shopping cart, loaded up with what I assume to be everything she owns in this world.

"Is that what this stupidity is about? Okay. I love you. Now will you cut the shit and come home?"

YOU HAVE ONE MINUTE REMAINING FOR THIS CALL. PLEASE DEPOSIT TEN CENTS FOR THE NEXT FIVE MINUTES.

I drop another dime in the slot.

THANK YOU.

"I got no one, Gina."

"What about me, Elaine? I don't have anyone either."

"God, you are so self-absorbed—"

"You have Chuck, and I have a new life. New friends. And they love me."

"Dropping out of school and living in the streets is a new life?"

"Any kind of life down here is a new life, whether I'm staying at the Ritz or sleeping in a dumpster. Any life up there with you, is no life at all."

A very long silence follows. Did she hang up? I'd be

okay with that, actually.

"Listen, Elaine, I gotta go—"

"It sure is lonely at the house." Her voice sounds quivery all of the sudden. "Found out what happened to you...that Friday at the Monkey Wrench—"

"Right, because the cops told you at the station."

"That night was…a blur...I don't remember much, Gina...I hadn't realized you took off, actually, until late Sunday night when I came home from work with Chinese take out for dinner and you weren't around. The Blums told me they hadn't seen you, but they told me everything...." Elaine's voice cracks.

She's starting to cry. But it isn't that sloppy, booze-induced, depressive—after she's had-too much-to-drink kind of crying—but a deep, earnest kind. A kind I've never heard come from her, except when Billy bailed on us.

"Elaine?"

No answer. I swallow hard.

"Elaine?"

"G...Gina...we have to talk...."

"I'm listening."

"I mean...really talk."

"I only have three dimes left."

"Not on the phone—"

"I'm not coming home, Elaine." I shake my head violently when I say this, looking much like the drunk dude across the street. He's pacing in front of Jake's Liquors, which is closed. He's shaking his head in stiff, jerky movements, like he's bopping to a beat no one else can hear.

"I won't have you living on the street—"

"I'm not living on the street, I'm staying with friends—"

"Who are these friends of yours?"

"I can't take living with you anymore!"

"I...I know—"

"Then why are we talking?!"

"Because you called me."

Right.

"If you wanted to be free of me, then why'd you call, Gina?"

To say hello. To check in....Of course I can't tell her this.

"You can't just be turned loose in the streets. I don't know who you're with...if you're okay...you don't sound okay."

The Trans Am with tinted windows returns. This time slowing to a crawl as it rolls past. The passenger side window comes down. A man with platinum hair and tattoos on his neck sticks his head out. He gawks at me, a moment, before the window goes back up. The Trans Am guns it and disappears around the corner.

"There's something I need to tell you, Gina. In person."

"Okay." My knees feel so shaky, I can barely stand. My eyes are glued to the street corner where the Trans Am had disappeared.

"Give me the address of the closest Western Union."

"I'm not doing that."

"You can take a day trip to Beckett. We'll grab lunch at Happy Fridays. We'll talk—"

"I'm not doing that—"

"Okay, so you're not doing that. You don't have to be a little snot—"

"You don't have to make this a big deal, Elaine. Whatever it is you gotta tell me, you can tell me over the phone. I promise I won't hang up. Really, I'm all ears."

"Is there a diner down there? One easy for me to get to? In a place that's not dangerous? God, I can't believe you're down there."

"Yeah, hundreds," I snort, rolling my eyes.

"Come on, Gina. Help me out."

"Well? I'm not living in Podunk U.S.A., this isn't Beckett...there's one near the Greyhound station, the Galaxy, I think it's called—you're not gonna send the cops for me, are you?"

"Seriously, Gina. Am I the cop type?"

"If you show up drunk, I'll walk out."

"Have I ever been drunk in the daytime?"

Many times.

"I won't be drunk."

Uh-huh.

"Two o'clock, this afternoon?"

"Fine."

"You'll be there?" Elaine sounds like a little kid.

"Yeah."

The change, rattling somewhere inside that steel box makes an empty CHA-CHING sound when I hang up.

Elaine is seated at a booth near the door, when I enter the Galaxy. She's dolling herself up with lipstick—a candy apple smear on those lips. She snaps her compact shut and looks up. A hint of surprise, worry, then disgust flashes in her eyes as she scans me from head to toe, her eyes resting on the patches and safety pins, holding together the holes near the crotch of my pegged jeans. I pause in front of the table, trying to decide whether or not she'd been drinking.

The whites of her eyes, for a change, are not blood-shot. In fact, they're white as cue balls, and her face doesn't have that waterlogged, dead fish-in-the-river look, like it usually does. And I don't see chewing gum lolling on her tongue. The gum would be a telltale sign of her having had a few.

I look away so she won't see my pinned pupils. I'd crushed and snorted a few more pills before coming here, and I worry that she'll notice my red and runny nose and make a comment about it.

"Your hair's purple," she says, then, scowling at my leather jacket says, "Why don't you take that off?"

I shake my head.

"Sit down, then. You're making me nervous." She spools strands of fiery hair that've fallen from her French twist around her index finger.

I flop down in the gold, vinyl booth.

"I hate your hair."

"I'm happy to see you too, Elaine."

"I miss those honey-blonde locks."

She hated those too. I know this because she was always calling them 'dirty-blonde,' in an irritated tone, like she thought they were drab or something. And she'd harp on me constantly to let her dye my hair red like hers, using one of those home-kits.

"Stan, that boy I told you about...he did my hair for me."

He put the purple in days after I'd moved into the squat, first using peroxide then Manic Panic. It faded quickly, even though we used a lot of Manic Panic. It ended up, after three weeks, turning this pinky lavender. This week, it's more pink than lavender, with my dirty blond roots showing.

Elaine offers me her lipstick but I shake my head. Reaching across the table, then, she tries to push my greasy, dirty hair out of my eyes, but I jerk away, shooting her a nasty look.

"God." She throws up her hands.

A fat-legged waitress with hair like cotton candy waddles over. Her name tag says, BETTY.

"Coffee?" Betty says this like KAWFEE.

"Yes, please," Elaine says.

"Sure," I reply lamely.

There's a silence between Elaine and I as Betty pours the piping liquid into our thick porcelain mugs. Elaine orders cottage cheese and a fruit cup.

"Just coffee," I say.

"Come on, Gina. You gotta be hungry."

"Well, I'm not."

"You gotta eat. You've gotten so thin—"

"I'm not hungry."

"How about a blueberry muffin, sweetheart?" Betty says this like SWEET-HOT. "They're fresh baked...or maybe you'd like a bran one?"

Betty can keep her bran muffins to herself. My bowel movements are quite regular, thank you very much. All I want is to drink coffee and to smoke cigarettes and to have this *outing* with my aunt done and over with.

"No, thanks." I slouch in the booth, wringing my napkin under the table, until, with my sweat, it falls apart.

"Bring her two eggs sunny side up and bacon, extra crispy, with white toast, extra toasty. Be sure to slather on the butter. Extra butter. She loves butter." Elaine shoots Betty a wink, her bracelets making a tinkling noise as she makes a slathering gesture with her hand. Clearly she's enjoying her chat with Betty...one service worker to another, I guess...but it sure does make me want to puke. She never put her childrearing skills to practice before. Why start now?

"Two eggs, sunny side, coming up!" Betty twirls away.

"Oh," Elaine calls after Betty, "And bring us some marmalade, too, will ya?"

"Coming up."

"Okay, Elaine, you don't have to pour it on...this nurturing crap's giving me the creeps." I roll my eyes.

Elaine lights a smoke. I do the same. Taking a deep drag, I stare at my filthy nails and begin digging at the chipped black polish.

The eggs arrive. Sunny side up the way I like them. Normally the yokes—two, shiny yellow domes, almost orange in color—if they're the brown-shell kind—would be a mouth watering sight. But today they're just too damn bright. They're probably city eggs. The kind that come in bleached, white shells and are shelved in pink styrofoam cases, and then trucked in from God-knows-where—eggs with yolks that don't have the slightest trace of orange.

The whites are burnt around the edges and runny toward the center, forming a ring of mucus around the yellow, sightless eyes, which gaze up at me as if to ask how it is that they came into being—if they came from chicken parents or if they were created in a science lab, and then told that the idea of them coming from chickens was a myth....

"Are you waiting for the second coming of Christ? Eat your food, Gina, before it gets cold," Elaine says, even though she isn't moving any faster on her cottage cheese fruit cup.

A man sitting across the isle, sporting a toupee, undresses Elaine from out the corners of his eyes. He ogles her fiery hair, pulled back in a French knot that exposes her delicate neck. Her mint-colored, off-the-shoulder sweater showcases her creamy shoulders, dusted with freckles.

"He's using you," she says, oblivious to the man in the toupee. "And he'll continue to use you. Use you and then throw you away—"

"Who?" I snort, pretending to be interested in the varicose veins on Betty's fat legs. She's by the cash register, yapping with the two cops seated at the counter, and seems to have forgotten the toast that was supposed to come with my eggs.

"That kid who painted your *hair*. The one you let fuck you every night in exchange for a place to sleep."

"We call it making love, Elaine." I shoot her a nasty look.

Elaine laughs bitterly. "What about the other guys you live with? How many of 'em are there? Do they call it making love, too?"

I feel my face flush as I toss my napkin onto the table.

"They're gonna hurt you because that's what men do, Gina...men hurt girls."

The toast arrives. I pull the crust off—white bread lobbed with extra butter—and then smear it with an extra coat of marmalade.

"You could end up dead. You don't know what the fuck you're doing. You're only fifteen—"

"Sixteen. My birthday was last week. Did you forget?" The bacon is burnt the way I like it, but it tastes like ashtray. I eat it anyway.

Elaine looks out the window, at the knots of trash along the curbs, swirling like tiny dust devils in the early December wind. Her expression is far away, yet the hard, afternoon sunlight glares through the fly-specked windows, causing her to squint. She doesn't touch her food, but instead scrapes the blob of grape jam welded to the edge of the napkin dispenser with her nail.

"Mary misses you. She wants you to come home." Elaine stops scraping. She rests her chin in her hand.

"So this is the big conversation you wanted to have with me?" I wipe the dribble of yolk from my chin with the back of my hand. I didn't realize I was so hungry.

My diet for the last month has consisted of bologna, an excellent source of protein, and government creamed corn, a fantastic source of fiber. The boys keep cans and cans of the stuff in the cupboards. They get it from the survival center, in the basement of a local church. We wash our meals down with glasses of Tang—a reliable source of Vitamin C—that tempers the chlorine flavor of city tap water.

"No, Gina, it's not...it's not the big conversation—"

"I need to use the toilet." I stand.

The tiny restroom reeks of Lysol and pink hand soap. I splash cold water on my face, realizing for the first time that my hands are shaking. So are my knees. Before this morning, I wasn't sure if my aunt and I would see each other again. Now I don't know what to say to her. I wish I could tell her stuff...talk to her about my life here...ask her things...stuff about Stan.

"I need so badly to talk to you, Elaine—without judgment," I mutter, my voice swallowed up by the cramped space, dim, due to the red light bulb at the end of a pull chain, and barely big enough to turn around in. I unbuckle my jeans and sit on the toilet.

Even in the red lighting I can see the blood on my underwear. My privates feel like they're on fire when I pee. It's been like this for a couple of days...pressure in my abdomen...itching down there and all that.

Elaine is reaching into her purse when I walk slowly back to the table. "Wait till later to look inside. Don't do it here." She looks embarrassed as she hands me a small, plastic shopping bag.

"Thanks," I mutter, warily taking it. For a second our hands touch.

"Watch my pocketbook while I go to the restroom." She forces a smile.

I look in the bag anyway. I roll my eyes when I see the contents: a box of ribbed condoms and a handwritten note:

PLEASE BE CAREFUL
DOWN THERE IN THE CITY.

When no one's looking, I steal ten bucks from her wallet. She returns fifteen minutes later, her eyes red as if she'd been crying. I feel like a heel.

"Wanna get going?" She fishes a wad of cash from her wallet, oblivious to the missing ten dollars.

"I thought we were talking?"

"We are, but I thought you could walk me to the car. "

"Walk you to the car?" Panic rises in my throat. I follow her anyway, dragging my heels as we leave the diner.

****

Outside, Elaine's eyes dart about, never once resting on any one person or thing for longer than a second. Clutching her purse to her chest, she bolts across 9th Avenue, pretending not to notice the hookers in hot pants, their faces shellacked with foundation as they lean into the windows of every parked car—except Elaine's brown Cutlass. The clunker is parked across the street from the Galaxy.

I hang back in front of the diner, noting how small Elaine looks among the tall buildings and afternoon shadows that splash the concrete. She whirls around, sees that I'm not there and looks wildly about, like a kid lost in a grocery isle. Her lips curl in a frown when she spots me. She waves her hand for me to follow.

I groan.

"One benefit to driving a junker," Elaine laughs a nervous, high laugh, her hand shaking as she unlocks the passenger door. "Is you don't gotta worry about anyone breaking in—"

"What're you doing?"

"What?"

"Why are you doing that? Unlocking the door? I'm not getting in there."

"I thought we'd sit a minute." Her eyes are bright and shiny and clear in the December light— smiling, even as they come close to shedding tears.

"You're not gonna get me into that car, Elaine. I know what you're up to, and I'm not falling for it."

"Conversation. Ten minutes. That's all. We needed the privacy—"

"We were alone in a booth. That's not private enough?" She should try living here. She'd know then that aside from being in a bedroom, a cozy corner in a restaurant is about as much privacy as you'll ever get in New York—here, you can never get away from people.

"I'm not gonna abduct you. Just get in." Elaine jerks a thumb. She looks so serious.

Part of me does want to go home, even though I know things would be peachy for about two days before the bullshit started again. I guess I miss the woods, too, and my bed—there's nothing soft about New York. And of course, I always think about Mary and her mother. I sent them an I LOVE NEW YORK post card, but haven't written since.

Elaine unlocks her side and gets in. I do the same. The food in my stomach churns like laundry being tossed in a dryer, not so much from the familiar smell of stale cigarettes and vinyl, so much as the memories that these smells bring—although it is warm and toasty inside, a break from the chilled air.

Elaine locks her door. I roll my eyes when she reaches over to lock mine. Surprisingly, I smell no booze on her, just a whiff of Love's body spray. The air between us feels thick, but maybe because of the tension.

She lets out a cry when a man in a tattered army jacket raps on her window, holding up a styrofoam cup. "What's he want, Gina?" she whispers, squeezing close to me on the bench seat.

"Spare change."

"Should I scare him away with the horn?"

I roll my eyes. Then, leaning over Elaine, give him the finger while shaking my head NO. Elaine bursts out laughing so hard, tears stream down her cheeks.

"You think that's funny?"

"No...I don't know," she snorts, still laughing that piggy laugh of hers as she dabs at the tears with a rumpled Kleenex.

The bearded man, unfazed by my rudeness, taps on the window of the next parked car. I lean back in my seat, my eyes getting heavy.

"I quit drinking," Elaine says suddenly.

My eyes flick open. I turn to her, but she's staring out the window, at the dumpster, at the mouth of an alley.

"I got out of detox a week ago. Chuck bought me a huge box of chocolates. Ya know, cause sugar's good for recovering drunks."

"You couldn't tell me this in the diner?"

"Sharon's quitting too, but she's not gonna do detox or anything. She's gonna do it on her own...I went out and bought myself a new wardrobe to celebrate…I got this new, scoop-neck dress with matching pumps…I got a manicure...but oh, Gina, it's hard, hard, hard. Everyday, I'm this close to picking up a drink," Elaine demonstrates the fact by pressing her thumb and index finger close together. "And I can't even channel my addiction by hitting on guys at the Wrench 'cause I'm indebted to Chuck. No other guy woulda stuck by me the way my Chuckles did. He's still drinking, though, and I told him I don't want that shit around, and I don't wanna smell it on him either, and I don't wanna smell Lenny and Squiggy anymore.

"Chuckles is staying at Buddy's 'cause we got

in a huge fight...all 'cause I put the snake cage out on the curb, with the trash. The snakes got loose...Lenny was found in the neighbor's crab apple tree. Squiggy was found under the car, trying to get away from the neighbor's Chihuahua...I just got so tired of smelling that damn snake cage...I swear those snakes were gonna drive me to drink.

"It's tough, ya know, fightin' temptation everyday, and I mean, what am I gonna do about work? Being around all that booze and stuff? And John Hanlan...? *Ugh.* Now that I'm sober, Gina, I can see what a louse he really is—maybe I outta go back to hair dressing. Whatta ya think?"

"I think that you are full of shit." I reach for the door handle.

"Wait." Elaine's grip on my arm is stronger than I would've expected. "We're not done."

"You mean, you're not done talking about yourself?"

"I quit drinking. Aren't you happy for me?"

"What do you want? A medal? What am I supposed to say?" I yank myself from her grip. "Glad you kicked the bottle. Now all you gotta do is dump Chuck. His brain's more fermented than a holiday fruit cake."

The color drains from Elaine's face.

"But even if you did that, I still wouldn't go home with you because you're trying to trick me. You're trying to get me to believe it's all better between us but I don't think you've changed...you think you're having this big talk with me, but I think you're hiding something...."

Tears well in Elaine's eyes.

"And I'm confused about how we are as a family—if you can even call us a family because you don't feel like an aunt to me...normal families don't act like us. Aunts don't treat their nieces like cronies—"

"When have I treated you like a crony, Gina?"

"I don't care that we're not a typical family. There's lots of families that aren't typical...."

Stan lost his parents in a plane crash when he was twelve. His older brother, Gary, raised him until he graduated high school, two years ago. Jeff, the same age as Stan, was home-schooled because his parents worked in the carnival and traveled up and down the East Coast. Danny was born into a polygamous family: one dad and seven moms. At five, he became a foster child, living in a family with ten other kids. Joni and Janis's father left their mother when Joni and Janis were five and ten-years-old. He started a new family, and has had nothing to do with the girls since. Mary's home life, I think, is ideal, but then even she has her problems. Her parents are so overbearing.

I'm not alone with my pain, but there's just one difference. My friends know their history, while I've never even met extended family, and I don't call a fat drunken slob and his pet boa constrictors, extended family.

"There's lots of broken families, but at least they have a sense of their own identity. I don't even have that—"

"Of course you have an identity, you're my niece—"

"Who am I to you?"

"I told you about me—Ellen—many times—"

"Ellen, Ellen, Ellen! I could give two sucks about that woman! She fucking left me. You're here. You dragged me here to talk, now talk!" my shouts fill the car.

Tears are streaming down Elaine's cheeks.

"I don't even know who you are, Elaine...." Now I'm starting to cry. "You're a ghost, wearing a mask...at least my new friends, who you think are scum, don't walk around wearing masks. Sure, I let them fuck me, but at least I know what our relationship is, what I am to them—and they love me!"

"They don't love you, Gina!"

"You're just jealous 'cause they think I'm beautiful!"

"No, Gina." Elaine shakes her head.

"You think you're the only one men find attractive?"

"Mary loves you and she doesn't walk around with a mask. Yet you abandoned her—"

"What's Mary got to do with anything?"

"Gina, please don't." Elaine grabs me as I try to leave again.

"Let go." I draw a fist.

"Okay!" She lets go of my arm. "You're right! You're right! I am a selfish mother—"

"A selfish what?" My hand slips from the doorknob.

"And I am full of shit...and I'm sorry!" Elaine is sobbing in a way I've never seen anyone do except in those black and white movies she likes to watch. But there's no acting here, and I wonder if she's been crying like this during the weeks I've been away.

"Elaine?" My hand slips from the doorknob. "Did you just say, 'mother' or am I imagining things?"

"I don't know what I said, Gina. I'm tired." She seems

not to see me.

I lean back and close my eyes. My bladder hurts and I feel warm all over—sickly and clammy—inside my leather coat. It's like I'm coming down with something.

"I'm lying again," Elaine mutters. "God, I make myself sick." She sighs.

I open my eyes. "About what? Elaine, we're all the family we've got. Talk to me."

"I…there's…God, this is so hard…I...I uh...I've been lying to you...for years…most of your life, actually."

My heart pounds.

"Gina, you know that photo you carry around?"

"Yeah."

"That's not your father. It's a photo I found in a jewelry box I bought at a Salvation Army."

"Okay...so it's not a photo of Roger. Then why'd you give it to me?"

"I thought I was protecting you—"

"So, there are no photos of Roger either. Let me guess, lost in the fire?"

"Please, don't get sarcastic with me. I'm trying to talk. So just let me talk. Okay?"

"Sorry. It's just that you're not making much sense."

Silence.

"Gina, at sixteen, I was raped…by my next door neighbor. His…my neighbor…uh...he's uh…"

My heart bangs in my ears so hard I think I'm going to have a heart attack.

"That neighbor…he's your father—"

"The neighbor what? What did you *say*?" I feel like hitting her. I mean, what an outrageous thing to say. Has she completely lost it?

"I am your mother. Aunt Elaine does not exist. Ellen does not exist. Roger does not exist. I'm really, really sorry, Gina." Elaine starts crying again as she rests her head on the steering wheel. All I can do is stare past her head, at the neon PSYCHIC PALM READER sign, across the street from the Galaxy. My hand rests on the door handle, slick with sweat.

"So sorry."

I shake my head. "Why are you telling me this?"

"Because it's true...because it's the truth. Because you needed to know the truth sooner or later—"

"What would you know about truth?!"

"I know I'm not the most honest person, Gina, but unfortunately, this time, I am being absolutely truthful. Please understand."

My hands shake as I run them through my hair. *Hair*....

"But I got my dirty-blonde hair from Roger—"

"No. You got your dirty-blonde hair from the neighbor—"

"And…you said Roger was always tripping and bumping into things, and that he's where I got my clumsiness from." Now I'm starting to cry.

"No, Gina. I was clumsy growing up. You got that from me. There is no Roger—"

"But you—"

"Forget it. It's the truth. I'm sorry."

"Why are you telling me this?"

"Because it's true—"

"Why are you telling me this?"

"Because it's—"

"If you say that one more time, I will walk the fuck out, and you will never see me again!"

Silence.

"I wanna know why you're making this up."

We sit there in silence for a while.

I let out a heavy sigh, then light a cigarette.

"I was ashamed." Elaine's voice sounds flat. She'd stopped crying. "I felt like I'd asked for it. I... he used to flirt with me, the neighbor, you know? And I was flattered...you know...that an older guy would pay attention to me...so I flirted back. Didn't see any big deal in it. I was a big flirt, that's all... and I was popular with the guys at school. I loved male attention because your grandpa never paid any attention to me growing up. He wasn't the huggy kissy type, neither was your grandma.

"One afternoon the neighbor asked if I'd model for him. He was a painter. Had a studio on the second floor. I was thrilled that someone thought I was pretty enough to want to do a portrait of me. But when he got me alone, he told me to take my clothes off. I didn't know he was planning a nude and felt funny about it, but then thought, hey, some of my favorite art books have nudes. Okay, no big deal…but then he…he…." Elaine's voice shakes. "Oh, Gina, I felt so gross. So dirty...I never told anyone, figuring I had no business going over there in the first place.

"When I found out I was pregnant, I was like, what do I do? There were no clinics. I couldn't get an abortion. I had to tell my folks about the pregnancy but I never told them about the rape. I told no one.

"I dropped out of school...in my day they didn't allow pregnant girls in school, which was too bad because I was at the top of my class and had plans for college where I would've majored in art history. Then, since I was no longer welcome at home, or safe for that matter, I went upstate to live with my friend Ruthie.

"Once I felt your little feet kicking inside of me, I knew adoption would be out of the question—"

"If you were so gung-ho about not putting me up for adoption, why have you never referred to me as your daughter?"

"Because referring to you as my daughter would mean acknowledging what'd happened. If I told myself over and over that Ellen was the one who'd had a baby by that man and not me, then I'd be okay...I could raise her....

"For a while I believed my own lie. But soon, that wasn't enough. I had to invent Roger. Because if Roger existed, then that son of a bitch neighbor didn't. Do you understand now, Gina?

"Once I started with the lies, I couldn't stop, and the more I lied the more I drank. At first I drank to forget about the past, then I drank so I could live with all the lies. Then I drank even more so I wouldn't have to think about what I was doing to you....

"Mrs. Blum really bawled me out, Gina. She made me think about a lot over these past few weeks, like the way

I treated you at the police station...I only have a dim memory of that night—if I told you that you got what you deserved, it was only because I was busy blaming myself for what happened to me."

I fumble with the door handle. It clicks open. The heavy door swings wide.

"Where're you going?"

I vomit onto the curb. She strokes my back as if to soothe me. I want nothing to do with her touch, but am too weak to protest.

She's staring at me, looking incredibly young and childlike when I slide back in, letting the door click shut. I lean back and close my eyes.

"Are you gonna be okay?" She asks in a small voice.

"Mom, huh? Is Mom what you want me to call you from now on?" I mumble. Elaine is all I've ever known. Auntie Elaine if I want to piss her off.

"You can call me whatever you want, Gina. What you think's best. What's most comfortable for—"

"I mean what the *fuck* do I call you?" my voice cracks. "Mom? Mother? Ma?" I snort with laughter, laughing so hard, I drop my face into my hands and start crying again.

"Well...you can just call me Elaine, as you've done all along. Nothing needs to change there. That's cosmetic...chump change, really...nothing to sweat bullets about—"

"Nothing to sweat bullets about...just call you Elaine, as I have all along...I wish you'd never told me any of this."

"I'm really sorry, Gina—"

"So what's his name?"

"I honestly don't remember—"

"I don't believe you."

"People blank when traumatic stuff happens—"

"What's his name?"

Elaine shakes her head. Her lips quiver again.

"What's the address? I wanna know where the fucker lives."

Elaine shakes her head violently, like the drunk guy I'd seen on the street. She lights a cigarette. The smoke trails are silhouetted in the afternoon light, now beginning to fade as the sun sinks lower and the shadows from the buildings grow longer. They kiss the hood of the Cutlass.

"He's probably gone by now. Why dredge it up?"

"Because I want to know who. my. father. is." So I can kill him.

"Do you forgive me, Gina?"

"What's his house number?"

"I don't remember."

"The street?"

Elaine shakes her head.

"Color of the house?"

"Will you hate me forever for having lied to you?"

"Color of the house?"

"I honestly don't—"

"Either give me something to go on, Elaine, or not only will I never forgive you but you'll never see me again."

Elaine mashes her cigarette in the ashtray. It smolders.

"There's a gully between his house and the one I grew up in. A creek runs through it. It's a small street. Eber something...Avenue or Drive, I think. It's in Queens. His house is white...mine was blue...."

I step out and slam the door, and am already ten paces up the street when Elaine shouts, "Gina, will you promise me this isn't the last time we're gonna see each other?" She's half in, half out of the car and yelling to me over the hood, her face flushed. Part of me wants to stick around to comfort her, but part of me wants to walk out of her life for good.

I continue up the street, even as I hear the door slam and her footsteps, now following close behind.

"Gina!"

I walk faster, not turning around.

"Gina!" Elaine sounds winded and desperate. "Gina, half of you might be him...Gina? Gina? Listen to me! Half of you might be him...but half of you'll always be me! You're my daughter! Do you hear me?"

I round the corner before dropping down into the subway station.

"Gina, come back!" Elaine struggles down the steps, clutching the rail. "Gina, I love you!"

A pop and a hiss drowns out her voice as the subway train clatters into the station. The subway platform quivers under my feet. I board the One Train. The doors bang shut before Elaine can get to me. She pounds the glass, but I only catch snatches of her red hair through the graffiti smeared windows. Folks on the train are not fazed in the least, even as she starts to yell and scratch at the glass, chasing the train as it rolls out of the station.

****

A train, running on a neighboring track, bolts from another tunnel like a bullet in a gun chamber. Going in the same direction, it bobs and bounces until I'm certain we're going to collide. I gaze through the window, at the handful of passengers on the other train. A black man in a suit reads the newspaper, while a Chinese woman leans back with her eyes closed. Two, bearded men wearing those funny pilgrim-like hats sit in those seats that face the windows. Beside them is a man wearing a leather cab hat. He has the same color skin and hair as I do. Another man with shoulder length blond hair and long side burns clutches the pole. He gazes into my subway car with a deadpan stare as I'm gazing into his. Either of these men could be my father for all I know.

Maybe its my nerves, but maybe it's because I'm feeling sick from whatever I've got going on down there, but I swear their eyes have become nothing but empty sockets. The lights of the subway car stutter off and on, off and on, off and on. Blue light splashes along the tunnel walls from the sparks, caused by the wheels grinding on the tracks. I squeeze my eyes shut, for a minute, trying to clear my head.

The men's eyes have returned to normal when I open

my eyes again. The other train switches tracks. It floats up, up, up, until all I see are grinding wheels as it slips into the dank throat of an upper cata-comb.

I pull the photo of my fictitious dad—a fictitious dad with dimples—out of my bag. I don't have dimples and neither does Elaine. How could I've been so dumb? The two passengers, sitting on either side of me, look on with a bored expression as I set the K-mart photo on fire with my Zippo. Together we watch the flames eat at the cheap, glossy finish. Together we watch them devour the face of a man I thought I at least kind of knew.

****

I walk the rest of the way to Eber Avenue, counting on the cool air to keep me sane—count-ing on it to talk me out of doing the stupid thing I'm about to do. Power lines thread their way through the upper branches of the Elms, connecting one lamp post to the next. A faint, sizzling noise passes through their umbilical chord thickness. If I focus on the sizzling sound long enough, I won't have to listen to my pulse pressing on my eardrums.

Keeping an eye out for the gully, I continue up the street, both fists jammed in the pockets of my leather jacket—my sweaty fingers curled over the half-smoked Winston in my left pocket, my sweaty fingers curled over the neck of a busted wine bottle in my right pocket. My eyes dart nervously from one side of the street to the other, noting that the snow had all melted, and that all the lawns look the same—rows of yew hedges and patches of natty grass, dotted with crab weeds, that divide one faded and peeling cape house from the next—1950s shoe boxes—way stations where folks go to sleep but not to live. I wouldn't've guessed New York City had places like this. I assumed the whole city looked like the Lower East Side.

Only one lawn stands out from the others. There's a FOR SALE sign among the overgrown grass, belonging to a slate gray Cape with a blue door. The windows are sealed with plywood. Vines bloom across the north face like varicose veins. To the left lay the gully, its water bearing a shattered reflection of the gray December sky. The water looks stagnant and brown from the fallen leaves.

This can't be it, can it? I glance at the FOR SALE sign, my mouth drier than a spool of yarn, my knees unsteady as I keep walking, hearing the hollow echo of the water trickling from a fat, rusted pipe running under the street. The chilled, November air pricks my lungs. I keep my fists in my pockets to steady myself as I reach the next house, white with a red door.

Parked in front, is a green Buick and a tricycle with streamers dangling from its handlebars. In the yard, a yellow-haired girl shrieks as she slithers down a plastic slide, on her belly. She pulls herself up off the ground. With her chubby hands, she clumsily rubs at the dirt stains on her pink corduroys. She smiles to herself while staring into space. In her own little world, she points at something in the trees that fascinates her and giggles. She smiles shyly when she sees me watching her. Her front teeth are missing. In a small voice, she says, "Hi."

"Miley, get inside and wash your hands," a man's voice calls from somewhere.

"Don't want to—"

"Miley! Inside. Now. It's supper time."

My heart catches in my throat when a man of solid build and a face white as the overcast sky, shuffles from the garage carrying a rake. The front door bangs shut as the little girl goes inside. I continue walking, then pass a few more dull, nondescript Capes until I'm cut off by a bustling cross street with a convenience store and check cashing place. Dizzy and weak in the knees, I sit in a bus shelter and smoke.

****

He's stuffing dead leaves into Hefty bags when I pass the house again—which might've been Elaine's, but then I thought she'd said that her house was the blue one, which is actually gray with a blue door—or maybe it used to be blue but had faded to gray—

"Can I help you?" His voice, lacking in bass, sounds friendly enough but guarded. Then again I am staring at the name on his mailbox:

GOODMAN

"Can I help you find something?"

My head snaps up. My face flushes. For all I know these are new neighbors—and who's to say Elaine isn't making this shit up? I glance at the tricycle. Rapists don't have families, Gina.

"Uh...I'm, uh...sorry, sir. I don't mean to be..." rude "nosey. I guess I thought..." you were a rapist. "Um, do you know where the closest subway station is? I need to get to Manhattan."

His eyes narrow as he leans his rake against the Buick and walks toward me. It's then that I notice the cleft—a deer print, branded in that sandy, stubbled chin of his. My heart starts to pound as my hand flies to my own chin.

I think about running, but my feet are anchored to the pavement, at the edge of his lawn, sweat pooling under my armpits, despite the raw December day.

"Do you know a woman named Elaine?" I blurt. "She used to live on this street—"

"Name doesn't ring a bell." His voice is so soft I can barely hear him, but the color starts to drain from his face. He frowns.

"She lived in that house, I think." I point in the direction of the boarded up Cape, surprised that I'm able to keep the shake out of my voice. My other hand remains in my pocket, clutched around the busted wine bottle neck.

His eyes become guarded as they refuse to look where I'm pointing. "I know no one by that name. His voice is more audible this time, but wooden. "The subway station's one street over." He jerks a thumb in the direction of the busy cross street. "You take a left at the end... and you keep on walking."

He grabs the rake and heads for the garage. The door slides on its track. He slinks into the shadows, and, not once looking back, lets the door rattle shut behind him.

I remain frozen in place, my heart pattering in my throat. The daughter smiles at me from the picture window. The shadow of her father appears next to her. Without looking out the window, he draws the curtain.

****

The glow from the street lamp never quite reaches the little white cape, now silhouetted against the dimming

176

daylight. The lights inside flick on, one by one, until all the windows, except the picture window, are lit by a soft, yellow glow.

Still standing at the edge of the yard, I chart his movements, watching as his shape disappears from one window, then reappears in another. I'm tempted to peer inside the kitchen window, to see how he lives.

'He was a painter. Had a studio on the second floor.'

My eyes rove to the second floor. He and his daughter now stand in front of the upstairs window, the window that I assume had been the window of the art studio. I'll bet the studio'd been turned into Miley's bedroom. He appears to be shaking something big and bulky...blankets? Is he tucking Miley in? Getting ready to read her a bedtime story?

'When he got me alone, he told me to take my clothes off.'

It happened, right there, in that small room under the peaked roof. Tears stream down my cheeks as I step slowly toward the house, until the flood light flicks on, startling me, and I duck in the shadows.

The upstairs window is dark when I look up again, and I suddenly lose my nerve. I back away from the house and quickly slide the note I'd written inside his mailbox.

So nice to finally meet you...

Dad.

At the train station, I reach inside my coat pocket for my subway token and end up slicing my finger on that stupid bottle neck.

****

By the time I return to the squat, I have a full on fever and no energy, and am glad no one's around. There's a loose brick in the wall beside Stan's bed, where he keeps his stash, but when I shine the flashlight in the hole, I find nothing. 'People sell drugs out of these abandoned buildings,' he told me once, and I consider going up the street, to a gutted four story where I've seen people buy drugs, but am too chicken. I'm used to the boys supplying me.

I search the zipper pouch of my Jansport, wondering if I might find at least one pill floating around at the bottom, but instead come away with the black, velvet box with the necklace. No wonder Elaine looked close to tears that day she gave it to me. Her behavior all makes sense now: those haunted moments of hers, her 'I'm sorry' presents, her lectures about staying away from the men, her inability to talk to me about sex and about family, her hostility toward Stan: 'He's using you...and he'll continue to use you...use you and then throw you away.'

Her distance toward me makes sense. Her treating me like a peer instead of family makes sense—being a product of her trauma, would she ever be able to truly love me? Sinking down into Stan's comforter, I hold the little black box to my chest and close my eyes, wondering what it'd be like to have Miley for a little half sister.

****

A hand, working its way under the back of my blouse, wakes me from a dead sleep. I remain frozen for a second, forgetting where I am. When I feel the hand work its way under my bra strap, I roll onto my back, my eyes darting about, fighting to adjust to the dark. A silhouette of a man lay along side me on the mattress, by the glow of the lava light.

"Hey." His warm breath brushes my face. His lips press into mine.

Too many hands on too many places and too many legs and too many tongues.

I swing my fists wildly. At first they connect to nothing but air, but I keep swinging until I connect with his body. My hands sting as they connect with his arms, his head, his face.

"Ouch! Fuck, Gina!"

There's a clicking sound as the bedside lamp comes on. Stan cowers by the table, next to the bed. He's touching his nose, now bleeding where I got him good.

"Want to explain what the deal is?" He laughs nervously, wiping his nose with the sheet as I roll out of bed and begin tossing my clothes into my Jansport bag.

"Gina, please tell me what I did." He sounds genuinely upset. Hurt flashes in his eyes.

I wish I had an answer for him. I grab my guitar and bomb my way toward the living room, the beam of my flashlight bouncing with every step, like the light on a hard hat.

I stumble into the hallway. At the top of the stairs, I clutch the banister, trying to steady myself as my knees begin to shake, but the banister begins to wobble, and I worry that I'll fall down the stairs.

"Gina! What's wrong, girl?" Stan pokes his head into the hallway.

From where I stand, I can only see the outline of his face, from the light of my Coleman, which I have pointed on him like a laser beam. For a second his eyes look like empty sockets set in a mask, a mask floating in the blackness. Squinting, he patters toward me.

"Don't you touch me!" I scream as he reaches out. He flinches.

Another door, opening onto the hallway, clicks open. There are sounds of shuffling feet. Danny's sleepy voice fills the hall. "What's wrong with Gina?" he asks.

"I don't know. She just started flipping out on me," Stan says as I get halfway down the top flight.

"Don't bother, guys. She's just some kid...let her go... we don't need the drama," Jeff's voice starts to fade as I reach the next landing, bawling as I nearly lose my grip on the rail, the staircase more narrow than I remember.

The battery on my flashlight starts to die as I hobble down the basement staircase, trying to avoid falling through the holes where steps used to be. I inch my way through the bowels of the building and out that narrow gap, leading me toward the light and the air.

****

Snowflakes, fat as pigeon feathers, spiral down from the night sky, now fading to a fuzzy gray as daylight approaches. Snow shimmers on the sidewalks, under the neon lights outside the Greyhound Station. Cigarette smoke curls around my pink-lavender hair, matted and damp from the weather.

I've been walking for two hours, chain smoking and shivering. As I step into a phone booth, I notice a boy around my age, across the street, strutting up and down 8th Avenue in just a thin leather jacket and mid-riff shirt that shows off his flat, hard stomach. His tight, pegged jeans really show off the goods. He smiles at the cars rolling past. A white Mercedes pulls to the curb. The boy leans into the passenger side window as I'm dialing home.

"Hello?" Elaine answers on the tenth ring, her voice groggy from sleep.

A tear slides down my nose and I draw in a quivering breath as I struggle to speak.

"Gina?" Her voice sounds anxious, yet hopeful. "Gina, is that you?"

The boy sees me watching him. Our eyes lock. For a minute he looks so sad. I understand his loneliness. He looks away, smiles at the driver and climbs in. The Mercedes pulls away. I watch the tail lights disappear among the heavy snow flakes.

"Hello? Who's there?!" Elaine cries.

"You're daughter, Gina. I'm coming home."

Amy Laprade received her MFA in Writing from Sarah Lawrence College and has taught poetry and fiction to writers of all ages and backgrounds. Her work has appeared in *Meat for Tea: the Valley Review* and *Canyon Voices*. "1405 Van Ness" won her an honorable mention at the Westmoreland Arts and Heritage Festival. "So Nice to Finally Meet You..." is her first novel.

You can visit her at lapradeamy@yahoo.com or LinkedIn.